NICE KITTY . . .

Growling, tail lashing, Pyramus moved towards the Inspector. He paused and roared an ear-splitting challenge.

As Pyramus started forward, I snatched up the sculptor's stand. Holding the stand in front of me, I tried to block Pyramus's advance.

'Get back! Back!' I jabbed the metal legs at him tentatively. He was a great, powerful beast. If he took another swing and connected with that rigid metal, I stood a good chance of getting a broken arm as the sculptor's stand was torn from my grasp.

Pyramus lunged and his teeth closed over one leg. He gnawed at it, growling viciously, then seemed surprised at the resistance his teeth encountered.

He gave a snarling roar and lashed out with a paw. . . .

Bantam Crime Line Books offer the finest in classic and modern British murder mysteries
Ask your bookseller for the books you have missed

Murder at the Cat Show

MARIAN BABSON

BANTAM BOOKS
NEW YORK · TORONTO · LONDON · SYDNEY · AUCKLAND

MURDER AT THE CAT SHOW
A Bantam Book / published by arrangement with
St. Martin's Press

PRINTING HISTORY
St. Martin's edition published 1972
Bantam edition / October 1990

ISBN 0-553-28590-4

Published simultaneously in the United States and Canada

PRINTED IN THE UNITED STATES OF AMERICA
OPM   0 9 8 7 6 5 4 3 2 1

Chapter

1

I can take cats or leave them alone—especially the four-legged variety. In fact, I prefer to leave them alone.

Not that they spook me. And I'm not an aureliophobe. I have absolutely nothing against them. It's just that they go their way, and I go mine. I'd always found it a perfectly convenient arrangement.

This time, however, quite a decent sum of money was involved, and so the twain were going to meet. Perkins & Tate (Public Relations) Ltd were contracted to do the PR for a glorified feline extravaganza, otherwise known as the 'Cats Through the Ages Exhibition.'

I followed Mrs Chesne-Malvern, the Organizer, through the Exhibition Hall, which was incorporated into one of Outer London's newest airport hotels, taking notes. I had the distinct impression that this was going to be my favourite memory of the whole Show. The carpenters and electricians were all over the place, the cats hadn't moved in yet. So far as I was concerned, the situation was ideal. It wasn't an opinion I felt safe in confiding to Mrs Chesne-Malvern.

'. . . and general interest,' she was saying. 'Here, for example—' she paused in front of a low platform with a half-completed railing high above it, from which curtains were obviously to drape—'we will have a replica of the life-size statue of Dick Whittington's cat on Highgate Hill. This has been especially designed for us and will be cast in gold by Hugo Verrier—perhaps you've heard of him?'

'I believe,' I said cautiously, 'we once did some publicity for his aunt.' I didn't add that she had not liked the publicity and had forcibly expressed her disapproval by raking a large chunk out of my partner's face. To add insult to injury, the picture of her doing so had made the front page of every paper in London. 'We got a lot of front page stuff,' I added truthfully. There was no point in telling her we hadn't been paid for it. We didn't want her to know a precedent had been established.

It seemed to satisfy her. 'We shall expect the same,' she said. 'You might like to note that the Golden Cat has been insured for £250,000. You might also like to note that it has genuine emeralds for eyes. Originally, they were a pair of earrings—my own modest contribution to Art. Of course, they've increased the value considerably—the statue itself is hollow—but one cannot put a price on Works of Art. And it *will* be an original Hugo Verrier, after all.'

'I thought you said it would be a replica of the Highgate Hill statue,' I said.

She frowned. 'Perhaps I expressed myself badly. It will be Hugo's own interpretation of the Whittington Cat. I can assure you, it will be a completely original Work of Art—within, of course, the framework of the Whittington legend.'

Hugo, was it? 'I see,' I murmured, and followed her as she moved hastily away from the low platform and led me to a heavily reinforced dais at the opposite end of the aisle. 'We'll have a statue of the Egyptian Cat-God Bast here,' she said. 'Genuine. We've arranged a special loan from a collector of Egyptian antiquities in the north. We are *not*—' she glanced at me sharply—'at liberty to divulge his name. Like most collectors, he prefers to remain

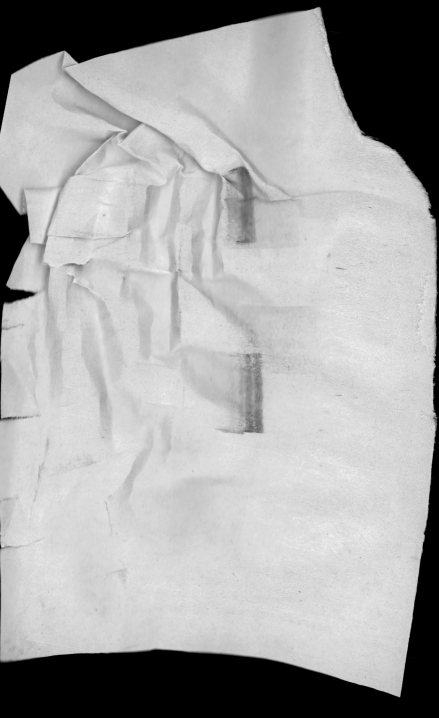

With thanks for the help and information received from:

The erstwhile Cat Information Centre
and
The Governing Council of the Cat Fancy
and especially:
Mrs. E. Aitken
Mrs. W. Davis
and
Mrs. G. Pond

anonymous these days. It's too often an invitation to burglary if it becomes known that one has a collection.

'Nor,' she forestalled a remark I hadn't been about to make, 'does he carry insurance on his collection, or any part of it. The premium would be prohibitive. In any case, it is invaluable and irreplaceable.'

I nodded, looking at the reinforcement of the dais. If the thing were that heavy, they were on a safe wicket about insurance. No one would be likely to pick it up and tuck it into a carrier bag.

'Now, over here—' we threaded our way back to the top and centre of the aisle, across piles of boards, wire mesh and electrical cables, to an ominous wheeled cage, facing down the aisle—'we'll have Pyramus and Thisbe. You've read about them, of course.'

'Of course,' I said. In the long annals of lady writers who had viewed unlikely mammals and decided *There's a book in you*, Pyramus and Thisbe were the latest to head the best-seller list. They were threatened only by the saga of a lady who had raised a boa constrictor from sickly babyhood. The recent revelation, however, that the lady had been a strip-tease artiste who had found a useful place in her act for her pet after the last fig leaf had been discarded— while sending the book to the top of the best-seller list in America—had weakened sales here in England, where animal lovers had been shocked by the thought of an innocent serpent being made party to a low theatrical routine.

In England, Pyramus and Thisbe—a beautiful, treacherous, and quite possibly deadly, pair of Sumatran tigers—reigned supreme. They would draw the crowds, all right. And the crowds would make them exceedingly nervous. For the first time, I began to feel exceedingly nervous myself. The cage didn't look all that strong.

'Have you any questions?' Mrs Chesne-Malvern shot at me suddenly.

Actually, I wanted to know where the bar was. But that didn't seem the sort of question an assiduous young PRO should ask during the first briefing, so I shook my head.

'You're sure?' She seemed disappointed.

'Well—' I remembered the clue I thought I had picked up earlier—'I think I might like to know more about Hugo Verrier—perhaps get pictures of the various stages in the creation of his Cat. You know— human interest stuff.'

She both smiled and frowned. I had the right idea, but had used the wrong jargon. However interesting he might be to her, personally, Hugo *was* human. And the whole idea of the Exhibition was that humans were to take a back seat to cats.

While she struggled with the words with which to correct me, I struggled with some words to extricate myself from the impasse. We collided in a dead heat.

'Actually, I think—' she began.

Just as I said, 'What I mean to say is—'

We stopped and grimaced at each other politely, each motioning for the other to continue.

Thanks to the rule of *Ladies first*, I won. After demurring graciously for a moment, she accepted the wave of my hand and continued.

'It was just,' she said, 'that I thought we ought to give extra attention to a special section we have in the Exhibition. *Working* animals. The Public so seldom considers them, you know.'

Her unconscious emphasis was interesting, as was the train of thought leading to the idea. So, Hugo, however artistic and brilliant he might be, was not to be classified as a working animal.

'Very interesting,' I said. But we were on the move again. I had already noticed that this area was more complete than any part of the auditorium so far. Ankle-deep red carpet lined an aisle between several large luxurious stalls, also well carpeted, with a corner of silken cushions in each spacious pen. We halted in front of a large cardboard cutout of a pair of shapely legs. At the feet, a fluffy white Persian lifted a gentle paw to stroke the nylons. She didn't need to tell me, but she told me anyway.

'This is where we'll have Lady Purr-fect—the Perfection Hosiery cat. It's largely thanks to Perfection Hosiery that we're having this Exhibition. You've seen Lady Purr-fect on television?'

'Of course.'

'You might like to mention—' she frowned at the paw lifted to stroke the nylons—'that she *is* perfect. I mean, she does have claws—and teeth—she's just naturally extremely gentle. *All* our cats have their teeth and claws. They've all been checked by our own veterinarian. We were most insistent about that—especially in the working cats section. After that unpleasant publicity a few years ago, we felt it was most important.'

Something seemed to be called for, she was looking at me expectantly. 'Oh, I quite agree,' I said hastily, establishing myself, I hoped, as a person of sensitivity in her eyes, although I would have been much happier to have heard that Pyramus and Thisbe had both been de-clawed and de-fanged. I wasn't at all pleased with their presence, although I could see that they were going to be one of our best publicity angles.

'And here—' we crossed the aisle to a fairyland boudoir scene—'we have Mother Brown.' Her face softened, her voice was almost hushed with awe.

I stared at the showcase pen, with somewhat less rapture than she. The coy little white satin bed was surmounted by a crown, from which fell half-draperies in the Napoleonic style. The initials 'MB' were intertwined in gold embroidery on the coverlet, and on the white woven matting of the stand. There was no clue to Mother Brown's affiliations, save for the miniscule scarlet lettering along the base of the bed, 'Keswick Catteries.'

'Very nice,' I said. 'Er . . . what product does she represent?'

'My dear man—' Mrs Chesne-Malvern seemed genuinely shocked—'Mother Brown is the product. That is, she produces it. Mother Brown's kittens are in the highest demand all over the world. In fact, you might say that Mother Brown is one of Britain's hidden export assets.'

'I see.' Well, that was a good line. And the stand was photogenic. We could probably give Mother Brown a bit of a knees-up, publicitywise.

'Actually—' Mrs Chesne-Malvern's voice lowered even more impressively—'we were extremely fortunate. Mother Brown will be here with her latest litter. Helena—that's Helena Keswick, of Keswick Catteries—wasn't able to promise in advance, but they just squeaked by at the minimum age for an Exhibition Litter. And the sire is Father Thames, also of Keswick Catteries. They're all sold already, of course. Helena has just kept them together for the Exhibition.'

And a lovely picture of dear little kitties, with their dear little Mum—of a sort to delight the flinty heart of any photo editor. 'That's fine,' I said heartily. 'Just what we want.'

'We're very pleased they passed the age requirement—' she glanced at me obliquely—'but Helena is usually good about timing.'

Was there a trace of acidity in that remark? I was tired, and it had been a full day even before I had decided to come over and case the joint of our latest client. There were moments when I felt I would be glad of a steady nine-to-five job in some dull firm with the same dull people, day after day. At least one wouldn't be perpetually trying to discover the lay of the land. One would know where one stood: in the same place, amongst people who would never change, and would uncompromisingly be the same, day after day. No surprises, and no interest. Further reflection along these lines always brought me back to the feeling that I had chosen the better part. But there were also moments, such as this, when I remained unconvinced. It was uphill work, trying to walk a tightrope amongst the established relationships of a group of people to whom I was always a newcomer.

'Then, over here—' we moved to an adjoining stand, tricked out with a megaphone, director's chair, and miniature camera—'we have Betty Lington's Silver Fir. A stupid little thing—'

I wasn't sure whether she were referring to the mistress or the cat.

'—but beautifully photogenic.'

The cat, I decided, optionally. On the back wall of the stand was a blow-up montage of stills of several of Britain's leading actors and actresses, each fondling, with varying degrees of ease, the same platinum Persian.

'She spreads her much too thinly, if you ask me,' Mrs Chesne-Malvern said severely. 'After all, she's getting on. And those looks won't last for ever.'

Once again, I was confused.

'The real money is in trade-mark stuff. But she's just spread her net too wide. *And* she's been altered, too. So, how much of a future is there for her?'

The cat again—I sincerely hoped. I tried to look intelligent—a task I felt increasingly beyond me. Perhaps I should have let my partner, Gerry Tate, handle this. It had never occurred to me to plumb his feelings about cats but, at this moment, I felt they *must* be warmer than mine.

I recognized that I was being unfair. I hadn't seen any cats yet—not the four-legged variety. But Mrs Chesne-Malvern was rapidly putting me off the entire breed for life.

'When do the animals move in?' I asked. 'I mean,

do you bring them in the night before? Get them used
to the whole idea before the Public arrives to stare at
them? Or do you just have them come in that
morning?'

'The working cats,' she said pointedly, 'will come
in tomorrow night. Actually, they'll be working here
the next day. Perfection Hosiery has hired them for
that day, so, of course, the general Rules for Exhibi-
tions don't apply to them. Working cats are in a
special category. Perfection Hosiery will be photographing 'The Purr-fect Year', their next year's calendar, here. Lady Purr-fect will be posing with each
of the working cats, and by herself, for the months of
the year. That will take care of that day.

'The day after that, will be the Exhibition proper.
Again, the cats will come in the night before, be
checked by the Vet, and settled comfortably into
their pens. The pedigree cats, that is. The domestic
cats will arrive on the morning of the Exhibition. The
pedigree cats won't be judged, they're just for exhibition, as are the working cats. The domestic cats,
however, will be given prizes.'

'That sounds fine,' I said, taking the line of least
resistance. I felt that, with any encouragement at all,
she'd spend a few hours initiating me into all the
reasons for everything. Which would be more information than I needed to know just to get publicity for
them. She seemed to expect me to say something
more, however, and I tried to oblige.

'What about the owners?' I asked. 'Where do they
stay while their cats are penned here?'

'The Committee—the owners of the Working
Cats—will be staying in the hotel. The hotel has
kindly made rooms available to us—' she waved a
hand—'in a corridor adjoining the Exhibition Hall,
so that we can be nearby. It was most kind of
them—even though they've just opened, the hotel is
fully booked. I suppose,' she added reluctantly,

'we'll have to acknowledge them in the publicity releases.'

'It would be the sporting thing to do,' I agreed. 'It's nice of them to fit you in, and so close to the Exhibition Hall itself. It means you can pop in and see how the cats are during the night, doesn't it?'

'You must remember,' she said, perhaps detecting something not quite *simpatico* in my tone, 'that these are extremely valuable animals. Each one represents a small fortune—both now and potentially. Of course, we'll have a Security Man on guard throughout, but it's in the hotel's best interest that the cats are as well looked after as possible. Also, these owners *are* the Committee, and they'd prefer to take no risk at all. They'll remain near their cats.'

'I see.' It was a new world, and I felt I would rather not turn around too suddenly in it, in case I saw the disembodied grin of the Cheshire Cat floating above one of the unfinished stalls. I *could* see, however, that the Committee had a vested interest in the Exhibition. You don't hire a PRO unless you have a vested interest in something.

They'd seen that Perfection Hosiery and Lady Purr-fect were in great danger of taking over the Exhibition completely, and so they'd brought in Perkins & Tate to do the publicity for their own Working Cats. The Lady Purr-fects (I'd heard there was a stable of them, all identical, and all doubling for each other like actors and dictators in a Banana Republic) were an industry in themselves. An industry geared to, and powered by, high-octane publicity.

The Committee, not realizing the ins and outs of the matter, would expect the Working Cats' publicity to equal, if not surpass, Lady Purr-fect's publicity. Otherwise, why were they spending good money hiring a PRO? The resultant space would be matched, line by line and photo by photo, with Lady Purr-fect's coverage and—inevitably—found wanting. But how do you explain these things to ama-

teurs? They think you're just concocting an alibi
before you even start.

'The Working Cats will move in tomorrow night,'
Mrs Chesne-Malvern said crisply. 'Oh, yes,' she
answered my raised eyebrow, 'everything will be
ready by then. Next morning, they'll start shooting
the calendar. At 12.30, television news cameras will
be here to take Kellington Dasczo unveiling the
Whittington Cat. Mr Dasczo is also on the Committee
and will be exhibiting his Pearlie King.' She glanced
at me proudly. 'So, you see, we'll already have quite
a bit of publicity from him—before you even start.'

I winced inwardly. No wonder we'd been hired, as
an afterthought. The presence of Kellington Dasczo
would practically guarantee that no one else in the
Press would give the Show a tumble. Kellington
Dasczo had parlayed his mother's indiscretion with a
Czechoslovakian pilot during the War into two pa-
thetic autobiographies of fatherless chee-ild, just as
soon as he had been old enough to realize the
saleability of the theme and change his name by
deed poll to the one he swore was his father's. In
moments when he thought he could get away with it,
he hinted strongly at a Title which should have gone
with the name—Count, at least. After that lucrative
mine had been nearly played out, he struck pay dirt
again by adopting a luckless alley cat and concentrating on *its* biography. This had gained him, apart
from great sales and lecture tours, a weekly column
in one of the soppier tabloids. And succeeded in
making Pearlie King nearly as despised in Fleet
Street as his master.

'You'll want to see the Press arrangements, of
course.' Mrs Chesne-Malvern set off at a brisk pace
across a labyrinth of abandoned timber and led the
way up a flight of spiral iron stairs. 'We have a Press
Box overlooking the Exhibition, with quite a comprehensive bar. The Exhibitors—' she sounded
disapproving—'will be using it for the duration of

the Exhibition, and a catering firm will provide sandwiches and snacks.' She opened the door and snapped the light on.

A tall, lanky man unwound himself from an easy chair and stood up, trying to look disassociated from the double brandy in his hand. 'Ah, there you are, Rose,' he said. 'I was just looking for you.'

'Were you?' she said icily.

'Yes, that is—' He stopped, and a distressed quiver shook him just before he sneezed so violently he nearly spilled his drink. His eyes, I noticed, were red-rimmed and watery. 'Sorry, my dear,' he said apologetically.

'Your allergy—' she was icier than before—'cannot possibly be bothering you. There isn't a cat in the place.'

'There must be . . . be . . .' he sneezed again. 'Either that, or there are cat hairs on some of the—'

'Nonsense!' she snapped. 'It's all your imagination—I keep telling you that.'

'But, my dear, the doctor—'

'He's a fool, and so are—' She broke off, remembering my presence. She turned to me and gestured in introduction to the man.

'My husband, Roger,' she admitted regretfully.

Chapter

2

Perkins & Tate were at the Exhibition Hall at 7.00 next evening. Gerry Tate brought the camera—it always reassures the Clients to see a camera. Penny, our secretary-assistant, had volunteered free-of-charge overtime, so that she wouldn't miss any of the fun. Since the price was right, we allowed her to come along and carry spare flashbulbs.

A giant Puss-in-Boots bestrode the front entrance like a feline Colossus of Rhodes. Huddled nearby, an anxious knot of children—two boys and a girl—stared up at it, and then at the sign on the entrance booth, which said, 'Children, accompanied by adults only . . . 25p: (5/-).' It rather surprised me, as I hadn't considered a Cat Exhibition an X Certificate production. On second thought, I realized that stray urchins darting through the Exhibition Hall, calling to each other, and trying to pat pretty pussy would make for a great deal of confusion and upset. It seemed tough on these kids, though. They seemed to be a serious little group, and they were taking the bad news pretty hard.

Gerry took a couple of shots of the entrance and we went inside. At first glance, there seemed confusion and kitty-litter everywhere.

There was a crowd at Lady Purr-fect's booth. A group of advertising types were setting up lights and cameras, while a few more brushed her fur, retied a satin bow around her neck, and all but sprayed her with perfume. She sat in the midst of all the attention, looking sulky and bored. I couldn't say I blamed her.

The next stall was occupied by a small, silver-haired man, wearing enormous silver-rimmed glasses, and a sleek, black tail-less tom with a nasty look in its eye. They were both regarding Lady Purr-fect's set-up with envy. Seeing Gerry's camera, the man hurried forward.

'Good evening, are you Press? My name is Marcus Opal—and this is Precious Black Jade, my Manx. Precious has won five County Cat Shows in just one year of showing, and done several freelance modelling assignments. We're expecting great things from this Exhibition, aren't we, Precious?' He reached out an abstracted hand to stroke the cat, still watching us. He should have been watching the cat. Precious laid his ears back and raked several inches of skin off Opal's hand.

'Precious is frightfully temperamental,' he confided, raising the back of his hand to his mouth and licking the scratches absently. 'But he's beautifully photogenic. If you'd like to—' He moved aside, so that we could have a better view of Precious.

'Actually, we're not Press,' I explained. 'We're the PROs for the Exhibition, but I'm sure we can use a shot of . . . er . . . Precious . . . for some publicity.'

Gerry raised the camera and aimed it. Precious crouched back on his haunches, looking like a miniature panther, and spat viciously. Gerry lowered the camera hurriedly.

'He seems to be camera-shy,' Gerry said.

'It's temperament—he's a very highly-bred cat and he has his little nervous crisis just before he settles down for every Show.' Marcus Opal stretched out his hand, and withdrew it quickly, as Precious raked the air with his claws. 'So high-spirited,' he murmured.

Precious turned in our direction and spat forcefully.

'Perhaps we should come back later—when he's settled down,' I said. Gerry was already backing hurriedly away.

In backing, he tripped over a suitcase.

'Oh, I'm terribly sorry,' Opal rushed forward and gathered up the suitcase. 'My case. I'll stay here during the Show. I couldn't leave Precious Black Jade alone. He's much too sensitive.'

Precious arched his back and spat again.

'I can see that,' Gerry murmured, still backing.

We were at the next stall now. A small, haughty Siamese stared at us coolly. A whisker twitched, as though in amusement. It seems silly to say so but, after Precious, there was something almost human about this one.

'Hello, darling,' Penny said softly. 'What are you doing here all alone?'

'Poor darling,' a warm voice said behind us, 'she's always alone. I expect she's used to it by this time. She's Pandora—Rose Chesne-Malvern's cat. Rose only keeps her to show—' the voice hardened with the animosity of the true cat-lover for those who care only for ribbons—'she boards her out the rest of the time.'

We turned as one. 'That's monstrous!' Penny said indignantly. I wouldn't have put it quite so strongly, but it was evidently the right thing to say, and not a bit exaggerated for a cat-lover.

'I agree,' the voice warmed again, almost purring. 'Most of us think that. Unfortunately, there's nothing in the Rules against it.'

The woman was rather like a cat, herself. A small face, pointed chin, green eyes that didn't quite slant, somehow all added up to a friendly effect. Especially when she smiled—the smile was rather devastating. It let us in on secrets, on amusement, on a different way of life. As though she were an interpreter who would guide us through the protocol of a country that was stranger than we had imagined, but not nearly so daunting.

Gerry—always the ladies' man—was reeling. 'I don't believe we've had the pleasure—'

'I'm Helena Keswick,' she said, extending her hand. (He nearly kissed it.) 'Of Keswick Catteries. You know,' her smile broadened, confided, 'Mother Brown.'

'Not really!' Gerry bluffed. It seemed to be the only possible answer.

It was so smoothly done I wouldn't have believed it possible but, without quite realizing we were moving, we had been led across the aisle and were standing in front of another stall. It occurred to me that she was probably quite a loss to the Public Relations business.

'Really!' The wave of her hand took in the stall. On the Napoleonic bed, a smooth, beautifully-groomed, reddish-brown cat lay peacefully, nearly submerged under a heap of slumbering kittens. Discreetly tucked away in a corner of the stall was a suitcase.

'You're on the Committee, too,' I remarked. 'And you'll be staying here during the Exhibition.'

'Naturally.' She turned to me. 'In any case, I wouldn't like to leave Mother Brown overnight. And Exhibition Litters can't be penned overnight, so they'll all spend their nights in my room with me. Naturally, I'm very pleased that the hotel has given us rooms so close to the Exhibition Hall.'

'Naturally.' Penny smiled at her, they seemed to have established an instant rapport. Well, it might be useful. But I had never suspected Penny of this fellow-feeling for cats. It made me mildly uneasy.

In the adjoining stall, at the end of the aisle, the immense granite statue of Bast towered over the booth benignly, and seemed to regard Mother Brown with approval. I blinked hard, and it turned to an impassive carving.

'I've never seen a cat quite like her before,' Penny said admiringly.

'There aren't *too* many around,' Helena Keswick agreed cordially. 'She's a pure-bred Burmese. Top of the Class.'

'I should think so,' Penny said. She hesitated. 'May I stroke her? I won't disturb the kittens.'

As Helena Keswick smiled, Mother Brown arched her neck to the outstretched hand, inviting the caress. 'Oh, you lovely thing,' Penny cooed, and dissolved into hopeless mush. It quite amazed me—I never would have thought Penny could get so soppy over a cat.

I mean, she seemed a nice enough cat—especially after Precious. This one was a sort of housecoat-and-slippers homely type; warm and friendly, but a bit too maternal for my taste.

I backed away slightly and hit against the rail separating Mother Brown's boudoir from the ersatz-Hollywood set next door.

'*Do* be careful,' a waspish voice said, 'you'll knock it down.'

I turned to apologize. The tall, thin woman, who must be Betty Lington, was cradling what looked at first like a silver fox muff. It wouldn't have surprised me, for she had a 1930's type face, with the thin arched-line brows and thinner, widened mouth. It was coming back into style these days, but one had the uncomfortable impression that, for her, it had never gone out of style.

The muff stirred and raised a head, becoming, unquestionably, a cat. Another type of cat. (It was beginning to worry me, the way they were all assuming personalities.) I had always thought a cat was a cat was a cat. But this one was a chorus girl cat, you could see it in her lovely face and empty eyes. She was beautiful, vapid, and hopelessly stupid. She would photograph like a dream, and never spoil a shot—but only because she was too basically inert to consider moving from wherever she had been set down.

'Silver Fir is upset enough with all this excitement, without your knocking the stand to pieces,' Betty Lington scolded. Silver Fir yawned. There was solid bone beneath that glorious platinum fur and between those pretty ears. It would have taken a bomb explosion before any intimation of disquiet penetrated her limited intelligence.

Nevertheless, the usual suitcase was in a corner of the stall. Like a fond parent, the cat owner was obviously the last to admit to any shortcomings of her darling. Betty Lington had decided that Silver Fir was an artistic and temperamental creature, therefore, she was going to stay with her and cosset her, even though Silver Fir couldn't care less.

The blue-white flash of Gerry's camera exploded behind us. Silver Fir merely blinked, but Betty Lington was instantly aquiver. 'They're taking photographs,' she snapped. 'Why are they taking that cat? Why aren't they taking Silver Fir? She's a film and television star!'

Stage Mother to a cat—now I'd seen everything. I should have picked up on the clue when Rose Chesne-Malvern was showing me around earlier. It gave me a strange feeling of impending doom—the last Stage Mother I'd met had been murdered.

'Do I scent publicity?' A low, purring voice sounded behind me, and I turned to face Kellington Dasczo. 'Doug, my boy, you might have started with an old friend if you were going to start photographing. Ah, I see Gerry's doing the honours—and you have the ravishing Penelope with you.'

He bowed, in his usual pseudo-courtly manner, to Penny, who nodded and smiled. We encountered him only occasionally, but that was often enough. He had obviously settled himself in his room first, and was now going to settle Pearlie King. He carried the famous three-legged high stool, which was Pearlie's favourite perch, under one arm, and a large black alley cat with a collar of little pearl buttons under the other. I wouldn't have given him credit for being so fond of his pet. No one would have—he was so fond of himself there was little love left over for any of God's other creatures. Still, Pearlie King represented a considerable investment already, and there were probably still several books and a good many articles left in him and his adventures. He certainly looked a lot more virile than his master.

'*You* get enough publicity,' Betty Lington said. 'Even if you *do* have to write most of it yourself.'

'Temper, temper, dear,' Kellington admonished. '*Some* people can be jealous without showing it. Much cleverer, really.'

'Jealous? Of you—?'

'Helly, Silly.' Ignoring her, Kellington stretched out a hand and patted Silver Fir's head. 'That's what they all call her, you know,' he confided to me. 'Silly. You can see why, can't you?'

Actually, you could. Great, blank eyes blinking with pleasure, as though she had been paid a compliment, Silver Fir twisted her solid little head to direct the hand behind an ear which wanted scratching.

Kellington obliged. While Betty Lington bristled wordlessly, he massaged the empty, photogenic head. From his arm, Pearlie King looked on with complacent contempt.

'Poor old Silly,' Kellington crooned. 'If only you had a brain, you might have learned a few tricks and gone on to character parts when you were too old to be just a pretty face.'

That was too much for Betty Lington. 'I'll have you know,' she exploded, 'that Silver Fir has just signed a new seven-year contract with Occasion Films.'

'I'm glad to hear it,' Kellington said. He assessed Silver Fir through narrowed eyes. 'Seven years—yes, that should just about see her out. *If* the Studio doesn't fold. There *have* been rumours . . .'

Before Betty Lington could reply, a thunderous snarling roar sounded over the background noise. Kellington's eyes narrowed almost to slits as he turned his head. It was a curious thing—but the eyes of the two cats also narrowed to slits. They all stared in the direction of the sounds.

They were bringing in the Big Cats. Something of the jungle came with them. The fetid smell of sated carnivores, a wild projection of rage at captivity. We watched as the travelling cage rolled past us down the aisle to the Exhibition Cage. The workmen pushing it along were pale beneath their weatherbeaten skins.

A tall woman stalked beside the cage, chirruping encouragement to the animals. Ignoring her, they paced the cage, snarling their resentment, pausing occasionally to claw through the bars, trying to sideswipe one of the workmen.

Swooping ahead, as they reached the end of the aisle, the woman opened the sliding door of the Exhibition Cage. The men closed the other cage up against it and she pulled a chain hanging at the side. A door slid upwards and Pyramus and Thisbe darted through it into the Exhibition Cage, and the doors clanged firmly shut behind them. So far, so good.

'I don't like it,' Betty Lington frowned. 'I don't care what she says—those animals are wild. A child could see it. They shouldn't be here, they'll upset the cats. I don't know what Rose Chesne-Malvern was thinking of.'

For once, we were all agreed.

'I hope she got good insurance coverage,' Kellington said. 'If anything should happen—'

Deep in his throat, Pearlie King growled warningly. Silver Fir looked at him in surprise, although even she had twitched as the cage went past.

'That's right, my beauty—' Kellington rubbed his

chin against the top of the stubby head—'you tell them. Let them come near your bailiwick and *you'll* have a go, won't you?'

Pearlie King lashed his tail and growled again. From across the aisle an answering growl came from Precious. Pearlie King laid his ears back and made a determined effort to wriggle out of Kellington's arms and meet the challenge. Kellington held tight, only a faint rim of perspiration along his hairline revealing how much of a struggle it was.

'You see,' Betty Lington said triumphantly. 'I told you it would upset the others. It's started to already.'

We were all pretty jumpy. The sound of wheels rolling along the aisle towards us again made us all whirl about briskly.

This time it was a sculptor's stand on castors being pushed down the aisle. The gold Whittington Cat was atop, gleaming in the artificial light, emerald eyes glittering, looking back over its shoulder at its creator, Hugo Verrier. Deep in conversation, Rose Chesne-Malvern walked beside him as he trundled the stand to the platform, lifted it on to the platform, and pulled a lever, retracting the castors so that the stand stood firm.

The flash of Gerry's camera caught Rose Chesne-Malvern's attention briefly and she glanced his way. 'You there!' She snapped her fingers, 'Come over here and take some pictures of this!'

I watched Gerry react. It's not that he minds having a bird snap her fingers at him, it's just that he prefers to have been introduced to her first. Apart from which, there's a way of doing it without offence— and that doesn't include addressing him as 'You, there.'

True to form, he ambled over to join us, turning his back on Rose Chesne-Malvern. 'That Mother Brown is a very interesting cat,' he told me. 'Do you know she starred in *Death Has Nine Lives*? The villain dipped the tips of her claws in curare and, when she

scratched her victims, they died. I saw the film, but
I didn't recognize her.'

'You, there!' Rose Chesne-Malvern stormed over to
us. 'I told you to come and take some pictures.'

'Mrs Chesne-Malvern—' I decided it was time to
straighten out some of the confusion, or attempt
to—'I'd like you to meet my partner, Gerry Tate.'

There was a flustered moment, while she tried to
decide what this did to the pecking order. She put
out her hand and murmured something, but seemed
to come to the conclusion that a partner in a Public
Relations Firm was still lower than the Organizer of
a Show who had hired him.

'Now, would you come over here, please?' She
threw in a tight-lipped smile for good measure. 'And
take some pictures of Hugo with his Cat? They ought
to go down well,' she turned to include me in the
grudging smile as she taught me my business—'with
the Press. The Cat is 18-carat gold, with emerald
eyes. Hugo will give you the statistics, height,
weight, and all that.' She turned and moved away,
with the bland assurance that we would follow her.

She was right, of course. Whatever we thought of
her personally, she was still the boss. Hugo watched
her approach. So, out of the corner of a slitted eye,
did the sleek Siamese, Pandora, in the next-door
stall, seeming to wait for some acknowledgment
from her owner of her existence, but too proud to
make the first overture herself.

Rose Chesne-Malvern stalked past her without a
glance. Pandora settled down on her haunches,
swirled the tip of her tail around between her front
paws, and became very busy washing it. I told myself
it was lunacy to want to kick that well-tailored little
rump on Pandora's behalf. Can a cat know that it has
been snubbed?

Gerry dutifully began taking pictures: the Whittington Cat alone, Hugo with the Cat, Rose and Hugo
with the Cat, and the Cat from different angles. The

curtains were hanging in place now. As soon as the picture-taking was finished, the Whittington Cat would disappear behind them, until Kennington Dasczo pulled the satin cord to part them for the television camera tomorrow.

After noting down the statistics Hugo had given me, I grew bored, and left them taking pictures while I wandered around some more.

Chapter

3

People were beginning to settle their cats down for
the night now. My watch said ten o'clock. Small
blankets had appeared from suitcases and were being spread in the Exhibition pens. I counted three
hot water bottles being carried to rooms to be filled
from hot water taps. These were then placed under
the blankets in the pens, even though the hotel
boasted about its central heating.

On the whole, the arrangements for the animals
looked quite comfortable, not to say luxurious. But
this was England, and such a state of affairs was only
to be expected. Remarks from passing tourists in the
lobby had given me an idea, though. An American
magazine might just go for an article about it, if I
shamelessly slanted it so that it might come into the
Quaint Olde Englande category.

I remembered seeing a not-too-uncomfortable-ap-
pearing couch in the Press Gallery overhanging the
auditorium. It occurred to me that I might spend the
night here myself. At best, I could get that extra
freelance story out of it; at worst, Rose Chesne-
Malvern would think that I was being a really
zealous PRO. At least, that was what I thought then.
Like a fool, I had no idea of what 'the worst' could
really mean.

I decided to reconnoitre the territory once more
and make sure the couch was as free from lumps as

it had seemed. (Not having an animal's comfort to worry about, I was damned well going to be concerned about my own.) At a stall opposite the staircase, I was halted in my tracks by a vaguely familiar face peering out through the branches of an unidentifiable shrub.

'Hello, there,' I said automatically. 'Nice to see you again.'

'I say—' the face broke into a broad public-relations smile and advanced a bit farther out of the bushes—'how truly spiffing to see you here!'

Since he hadn't thrown it at me in the first sentence, I gathered he couldn't remember my name, either.

'I didn't realize you were handling this Show.' A body, on hands and knees, began to emerge behind the beaming face.

'That's right.' At least, he knew my occupation, so he was one ahead in the game, although I had a hazy notion he was probably in advertising. 'This your stand?'

'It certainly is. Best new product on the market.' He stood up and let me have it straight between the eyes. 'Pussy No-Poo. The new, antiseptic, and guaranteed completely odourless once-a-week change for your litter box.'

I'll give him that, he said it with a straight face and without the trace of a wince or a smirk. I began to realize that this might be a boy to remember—if I could ever find out his name.

'Actually,' he went on, 'you could probably let it go for two weeks—but we don't like to say so. It might come under extravagant claims and, cats varying, and the new Advertising Act being what it is . . .' He trailed off and shrugged.

I nodded gravely. I was in no position to cast the first stone—we never could tell what our own next account might be. 'And, is this—' I gestured to the rather strange greeny-beige pseudo-soil, about two feet of which was embedding the shrubs and plants—'your . . . er . . . product?'

He knew I hadn't been able to bring myself to say it, but he forgave me. 'Pussy No-Poo,' he said unemphatically. 'That's right. That's just what it is.' He gestured to it, too, then seemed to realize that he was still holding his gardening equipment—a small three-pronged claw in one hand, and a trowel in the other. He shrugged apologetically, and dropped them beside a shovel and pitchfork already lying on the turf.

'They'll be bringing out a similar product for dogs in the near future. We should be able to introduce it in time for Cruft's.'

'Have they named that one yet?'

'The jury is still out, but it will probably be something equally nauseating,' he admitted.

'You say it very well.'

'Actually, there's a trick to it,' he said. 'One simply stands in front of a mirror and repeats the words over and over again, until they lose all meaning. It becomes a mere collection of syllables.'

I had been right, what's-his-name, here, *would* bear watching. 'Are you on duty for the whole Show?'

'Every bloody day of it. Three entire days telling cat owners all they want to know about our glorious product. And you?'

'I was thinking of signing on for the night shift right now, as a matter of fact.' I decided it was time to throw him a clue. 'Perkins & Tate are ever on the job.'

'Especially Perkins,' he grinned, catching it neatly. 'At least Rutherland Advertising doesn't demand the last full measure of devotion from its minions,' he reciprocated. 'So, it's home to a comfy bed for Dave Prendergast.'

'I was on my way up to the Press Gallery to check

the situation. It seems to me I noticed a couch up there the other day.'

'Right you are. Come and have a drink first.'

It seemed like a good idea. A much better idea than going upstairs and trying to sleep. The more I thought that one over, the more insane it sounded. But I reminded myself of the fees a nice human-interest article about cat-lovers might bring from an American magazine and, by the third drink, it seemed like a good idea again.

We said good night after the barmaid called 'Time,' and Dave hopped on a bus back to his flat, while I returned to the Exhibition Hall.

I sauntered along, in no hurry, enjoying the evening, and my eye was caught by a slogan scrawled in chalk on the side of the building, 'CHAMP IS OURS.' I regarded it with mild interest. I could swear that it hadn't been there earlier. As graffiti, I had seen wittier; but there was the ring of genuine protest about it. I wondered if Champ was a colony—like so many, of whose existence I had been unaware—or whether it was the initials of some new Protest Group.

Musing over the possibilities of the initials, I entered the Hall, skirting around the aisles of empty pens the other cats would occupy when the Exhibition got under way.

I found the stairs to the Press Gallery and climbed them quietly. Perhaps, if I had been less lulled by the past pleasant hour in the pub, and the peacefulness of the scene below, I might have been more on guard. But who would have expected that sort of thing amongst a group of respectable animal lovers?

So, I did what I had been brought up never to do, and entered a room without knocking. Fortunately, I didn't snap on the light. Something warned me just in time—perhaps the fresh smell of pipe tobacco in a dark room which should have been empty for hours.

I heard the couch creak and saw the faint glow of

a pipe and a cigarette in cosy proximity. It struck me as definitely a moment when discretion was the better part of valour. Certainly, it was no time to stand there in the doorway and blurt out an apology.

I backed out of the room hastily and closed the door behind me, then bolted down the stairs three at a time. I stood at the foot of the stairs, uncertain of my next move. If I walked out into the hall, I would be visible from above, and they would know who had stood in the doorway. The situation was embarrassing enough without that. Perhaps they would prefer to know who it had been, rather than look at every person they met and wonder if that was the one; but I would prefer not to be pinpointed as the intruder.

A muffled growl made me leap nearly out of my skin, until I realized it must be Pyramus, or perhaps Thisbe. I was standing next to their cage, which was beneath the overhanging Press Gallery. There, at least, was a move I could make without being observed from above.

I ducked under the guard rail, circled to the front of the cage, and stared in at them abstractedly. They were both asleep, tumbled together like the more domestic variety of cat. Evidently one had been having a dream which had evoked the growl. He, or she, was twitching spasmodically. They were a pretty, graceful sight—so long as one was on the outside looking in.

'Aaah.' It was almost another growl. I leaped again, but it was a low voice at my elbow. 'They are beautiful in slumber, are they not?'

I turned to face two tigerish eyes on a level with my own. 'I can see that you have a soul.' The eyes bored into mine intensely, and I resisted a nervous impulse to deny everything—especially that I had a soul.

'It is very important, I feel, for a veterinary surgeon to have a soul.'

'I suppose it is,' I said, 'but I happen to be the Public Relations Officer.'

'Aaah?' Her eyes narrowed and there was a long silence while she assimilated this new information. She stared thoughtfully at her cats, leaving me free to stare at her.

Her jet black hair was a heavy coil at the base of her neck. The dark face, with its slanted tawny eyes, and odd planes, might have belonged to an ancient Aztec or Inca princess. Or, more likely, High Priestess.

There was quite a lot of the jungle about her, as well as about her cats. It was easy to imagine her gliding through a jungle with that silent, feline walk of hers, her colouring blending in with the foliage. In fact, she had. I began remembering newspaper stories from my childhood.

In the drab post-war austerity years, she'd brightened many a front page. A remote revolution, with a fiery Latin beauty rallying the front lines to the charge, seemed a lot more glamorous than the late unpleasantness. There'd been a lot said—both for and against her. But once she'd caught the bullet she'd seemed to be seeking, everything was forgiven her—even by her enemies.

Truce had been declared over her recumbent form and both sides had joined in fighting for her recovery. From a midnight operation in a guerrilla tent, she'd been flown to a private room in the best hospital in the capital city. Both factions met—fairly amicably—while visiting her.

Taking advantage of the fact that she was too weak to put up much resistance, her Old Guard family had arranged a marriage with an older suitor, whose brilliant record in the Diplomatic Corps proved him a man exceptionally gifted at dealing with potentially explosive situations. Since the revolution had petered out by the time she'd recovered, Carlotta had surrendered to the inevitable with a minimum of

fireworks. A grateful Government had promptly be-
stowed several medals upon the intrepid Señor Montera and posted the happy couple to the fleshpots of
European Embassies, where the flash-point of local
insurgents was considered beyond Carlotta's range.
There had been periodic rumours, however, that she
still kept trying.

'These cats—' she turned to me abruptly—'you
believe in them?'

I hesitated, unsure of what sort of revolution I was
being invited to sign on for. 'Well,' I said tentatively,
opting for misunderstanding, 'they're here, aren't
they? I mean, it's not a question of belief or disbelief,
they're definitely, corporeally, *here*.' I wondered if
I'd be having this conversation if I hadn't spent so
long in the pub with Dave.

'Anyway,' I said, weakening my position still
further, 'I don't have to believe in them. All I have to
do is get publicity for them.'

'Aaah!' She stared at me, as though trying to assess
my suitability as a pawn in whatever plot she was
presently hatching. 'Then, for you, the golden cat
is the best.'

For someone so hung about with gold and jewels,
she sounded pretty contemptuous about the precious metal. Her engraved necklet alone must have
had a high intrinsic value and, I suspected, considerable value as an antiquity, as well. But that faint
contempt wasn't surprising, really, considering the
conditions of her native country. Although dictators
and their supporters are often accused of using their
wives as display cases for their wealth, the ladies are
actually travelling bank vaults. The Monteras could
have lived quite comfortably from the sale of Carlotta's jewels if revolution had cut off the revenue from
the family holdings. A lady doesn't get sentimental
about jewellery in those circumstances.

'The gold cat is just a gimmick,' I said. 'I don't
think much of it. The living cats are the Show.

They're what the Public will come to see. Any one of
them is worth more than the gold cat.' I spoke with
conviction, realizing I meant it, although I hadn't
consciously considered the issue at all.

'You are right!' She sounded almost surprised
about it. 'All living cats are greatly important. But
my cats are even more *importante* than these
others—they have intelligence, personality, fire!'

I was prepared to believe the last one. I nodded.
Which was foolish of me, it encouraged her.

'Come.' She took my hand and drew me nearer the
cage. 'Come and make friends with them. We will go
inside and I will introduce you.'

'No, thanks,' I said. 'Perhaps some other time.'
She wasn't getting me into that cage while I was still
alive and kicking. Although her book had insisted, in
the teeth (and claws) of all the evidence, that the
orphaned cubs she had rescued from an unfeeling
English Zoo were as tame as kittens, I didn't believe
it. There were too many photographs of loyal Latin
servants, wearing strained smiles and bandages, to
add real credence to her claim.

'You are afraid!' she challenged.

'Terrified,' I agreed, leaving the gauntlet where she
had flung it.

She didn't like that. In her native country, men had
plunged impetuously to their deaths for her, rather
than admit to a healthy normal nervousness. Certainly, if they were forced into the admission, they
weren't cheerful about it. She resorted to the goad.

'You are a coward!'

'Craven.' I tried an old joke. 'In fact, it's my
religion. I'm a devout coward.'

I might have known she wouldn't smile. These
things weren't to be joked about in jolly old Latin
wherever-it-was. Once you lived South enough of
the Border, you packed your sense of humour away
in mothballs, and took out the duelling pistols.

She smouldered at me, baffled. She never had

learned to ignite the damp squib of Anglo-Saxon temperament. It was stalemate, and neither of us could quite be the first to break away, although she obviously wanted nothing more to do with me. And it was mutual. I now had every sympathy for her native country. Although, libel laws being what they were, a word like 'exile' had never been mentioned in connection with the Monteras, I quite saw why they'd never been stationed in any Latin countries, nor invited home for many visits.

'Doug.' Someone had come up behind us. I whirled around and was relieved to discover Kellington Dasczo.

'Kellington!' I greeted him with a warmth he was not accustomed to. 'I didn't realize you were still up.'

'It's not even midnight,' he said defensively. 'I'm not used to such early hours. I began to think I was the only person left awake—left alive—in the entire world.'

'At least, in the Cat World,' I said. 'I thought cats were nocturnal animals. I never expected to find them going to bed with the chickens.'

'Left to themselves, they're fairly nocturnal,' he said. 'These are pampered pets, corrupted specimens. Tame as their owners—and as dull. Pearlie King can't sleep, either,' he added.

'Nor can I,' Carlotta said. 'I shall return to my apartment. There is still much to be done this night.' Her brooding eyes swept from the tigers to us and back again. 'Much.'

The night was young, and there was still time for a bit of rifle practice before dawn, I presumed.

'Don't let us keep you,' Kellington said.

'Do not stay here longer,' she commanded us. 'I will not have my cats disturbed. They must be fresh for the photographers in the morning.'

Lucky photographers. We nodded and watched her stalk down the aisle, back to her own lair. She was having no nonsense about moving into a strange hotel room in order to keep watch over *her* cats, and I saw her point. No one in their right mind would ever try to nobble, or make off with, one of them.

'There probably isn't a word of truth—' Kellington turned to me—'in the rumour that she feeds her ex-lovers to them.'

'I wouldn't like to bet on it,' I said.

'Like calls to like.' He surveyed Pyramus and Thisbe moodily. 'No wonder she chose a couple of man-eaters for her pets.'

I had been thinking something of the sort myself, but was getting too tired to sit down and have the kind of gossip Kellington regarded as analysing a situation critically.

'I'd thought I might stay the night,' I said, 'but the hotel is booked out and even the Press Gallery appears to be occupied. Perhaps I ought to be getting along . . .'

'There's a spare room going begging there.' He pointed towards the door opening into the corridor of Committee bedrooms. 'Rose Chesne-Malvern won't be using it. Catch *her* spending the night with a lonely, frightened cat. She's another one with better things to do. She won't mind if you use Room 121—she won't even notice.'

He sounded pretty sure. And he had a reputation in The Street of knowing his facts, even if he did present them in a particularly bitchy way. I wondered if it had been Rose Chesne-Malvern I had surprised in the Press Gallery—and who was with her? Hugo Verrier, perhaps, they had seemed quite friendly.

Kellington was looking at me expectantly. But, again, it was something I was too tired to rise to. This Exhibition was going on for two more bloody days. Somewhere, during that length of time, I was undoubtedly going to be backed off into a corner for a long cosy chat. But, not tonight, Kellington!

'Thanks,' I said, 'that's a very good idea. I think I will. Good night.'

As I entered the room, I saw twin pinpoints of light reflected in the pair of eyes watching me. Pandora, nose up against the bars of a carrying case on the bedside table, wasn't sleeping, either. I was too tired to wonder what she was doing there. Possibly Rose Chesne-Malvern had been intending to stay the night and had brought her in here before changing her mind.

'Don't let me disturb you.' I felt foolish, talking to a cat, but she was watching me so intently it seemed churlish to ignore her. 'I'm just going to get into this bed and snatch a few hours' sleep. Is that all right with you?'

She blinked indifferently and watched between half-closed eyelids as I took off my shoes and tie, loosened my collar and belt, and got into bed. I was quite unprepared for an overnight stay, but reminded myself that these few hours of discomfort might pay dividends. I was on the spot and would surely wake if anyone went cat-comforting in the night. Also, I would be first on deck in the morning when the photographers arrived to begin shooting the Purr-fect Year.

I had settled down and begun to feel that sleep might be around the corner. I was just relaxing into a doze when the bed swayed slightly. I opened my eyes in alarm, and found myself gazing into a pair of slanted blue eyes.

'What the hell are *you* doing here?' I muttered.

She widened her eyes and glared at me—as affronted as if *I* had crawled into *her* bed, instead of the other way round.

'How did you get—?' I broke off. The cage door had been fastened by a simple latch device, not really proof against the manoeuvring of a clever paw. It dawned on me why she had been named Pandora.

She was still standing at my shoulder, with the air

of an affronted dowager. I could get up and return her to her cage, but that was no guarantee that she would stay there. Besides, I was too close to sleep to care.

'Oh, hell.' I surrendered. 'All right. Just as long as you don't snore.'

She settled into the hollow of my neck and shoulder, her small silky head snaked beneath my chin. I lifted my head and wriggled about a bit, readjusting the blanket, until we were both fairly comfortable.

After a few moments, I felt the tiny muscles relax. As I drifted off to sleep, I noticed one point.

She didn't snore. She purred.

Chapter

4

I dreamt there was a bridge party in the next room. For some reason, I was half asleep on the bed and the ladies had all piled their fur coats on top of me. The party was getting noisier by the minute, and I seemed to have a mouthful of someone's mink.

I spat out the mink coat and pushed it away. It promptly snuggled back. I pushed it again and it seemed to take exception to this. It grew sharp-pointed teeth and sunk them in the lobe of my ear. This brought me sitting upright, and the mink grew claws and climbed my chest as I sat up. It perched on my shoulders, snarling softly at me for having disturbed it.

'Why, Mr Perkins,' a female voice said pleasantly, 'I didn't realize you were fond of cats.'

My eyes were open and beginning to focus. Helena Keswick was standing in the doorway, smiling down at me. There seemed to be something about the nightmare I couldn't shake off—something on my shoulder. I swam a little farther back to reality and realized I was sitting up in a strange bed, with Pandora clinging to a precarious hold on my shoulder. I began to regret that suits no longer had the heavy shoulder pads that were once fashionable.

'I'm so pleased to know that,' Helena Keswick said. 'It looks as though Rose Chesne-Malvern may have done the right thing—for once. It would have

been just like her to have hired Public Relations
people who hated cats.'

Since I felt I was rapidly getting to that state
myself, I didn't trust myself to speak. I simply
smiled. If I was a trifle tight-lipped about it, she
didn't know me well enough to notice.

'Since you're getting along so well with Pandora—' she put a couple of tins and a carton of milk
down on the table in front of the cage—'could I leave
you to feed her? I must get back to Mother Brown.'
She sailed away before I could answer.

I looked after her. Helena Keswick was wearing
a long, doubtless warm, but undoubtedly clinging,
nylon jersey housecoat over matching pyjamas, and
looking more than ever like a sleek feline. I wouldn't
have minded a mouthful of her fur.

Pandora gathered herself and took a flying leap
from my shoulder to the table. She nosed hungrily at
the tins and turned her head to glare at me impatiently. 'Mrryah!' she ordered.

I got up slowly. That was a female for you every
time. Out of the goodness of your heart, you let them
sleep with you—and then they thought they owned
you.

'Mrryah!' I wasn't moving fast enough. But the way
I felt, I was lucky to be moving at all. All I wanted
now was to get back to the flat, shower, shave and
change.

'Mrryah!' But my British training prevailed. The
livestock must be fed first. Perhaps because they
nagged so much.

There was a tin opener amongst the oddments in a
hamper under the table. I opened the tin with the
orange label—from the way Pandora was nosing at it,
that was the one she preferred—and wrestled with
the three-cornered milk carton a while before managing to twist a corner off without spilling too much.
I poured some into Pandora's bowl then, feeling that
fair was fair, took a swig myself. It wasn't as good as

hot coffee, but it helped a bit. I began to feel more awake, and less like something the cat had dragged in.

Pandora finished her breakfast and I decided to return her to her pen in the Exhibition Hall before doing anything else. I'd get her settled before the photographers arrived. I picked her up and carried her down the corridor to the Hall.

Looking around, I began to feel cheered. I wasn't in this boat alone. I nodded across the aisle to Kellington Dasczo, reflecting that I knew characters who would have paid good money for a sight of him, tieless, sprouting whiskers which were several shades darker than his hair, and tottering towards the Gents with Pearlie King's earth box to empty.

'Good morning, Mr Perkins,' Betty Lington sang out to me. Marcus Opal waved to me when I glanced his way. From all sides, I sensed an aura of approval. Now that I had stayed the night, it seemed that I had in some way proved my good faith. I was no longer an outsider paid to do the Public Relations, I was one of the gang.

Perhaps it had been worth the price of admission, after all. I was still reasonably young and in fair condition. My muscles would probably untie themselves again one day. Probably.

The cage door was swinging loosely. Pandora pawed it open and stepped inside. She walked over to her earth box, then paused and looked dubiously at the thin covering of gravel inside. I must say I agreed with her.

'Just hang on a minute,' I said. 'We can do better than that.'

I nipped around to Dave Prendergast's stall and filched a trial size packet of Pussy No-Poo. Pandora was still standing there, eyeing the earth tray with distaste, when I returned. I tore open the packet and emptied it into the earth tray, spreading it out evenly. Pandora stepped forward, sniffed inquiringly, patted

it with a paw, then got into the box. I decided Dave
could chalk the cost of the packet up to Market
Research—the product was now consumer-tested.
And approved.

The activity at Lady Purr-fect's stall was brewing
up to fever-pitch. Innumerable characters with cameras, floodlights, light meters and associated equipment, were dancing about.

'I'm still not happy about January,' I heard one of
them say.

'We don't have to shoot in sequence,' someone
soothed. 'Why not start with something else? How
about April?'

'I don't *feel* like April this morning.'

I was with him there—who among us did? A cold,
grey, bleak November was what I felt like. But I
didn't think I had a vote in the matter, so I kept quiet.

'June,' he decided arbitrarily. 'June and July, we'll
start with. We can use that arbour with all the trees
and bushes, down at the end. Quick now, before we
lose the mood.'

Before someone arrived to prevent them from
wrecking Dave's stall, he meant.

They swooped on Betty Lington's booth, collecting
Silver Fir and, of necessity, Betty Lington herself. I
followed along behind them, to watch the chaos. It
always cheered me to see other people trying to work
against the odds.

They took a few 'cute' shots, then proceeded to get
even cuter. 'Why don't we put one of them up a tree
and have the other one sitting at the foot looking up?'

'Not Silver Fir,' Betty Lington bristled immediately. '*She* doesn't risk her neck up in some tree.'

The camera crew exchanged glances, but obviously weren't feeling hardy enough to make an issue
of it. Not when Lady Purr-fect was on hand and
without a champion. One of the men picked her up
and started purposefully towards a medium-sized

sapling. Betty Lington allowed Silver Fir to be positioned at the foot of the tree.

Neither of the cats was particularly bothered. They were pretty evenly matched: it was an inert force and an immovable object.

Just then, the sapling tilted and Lady Purr-fect lost ground by putting out her claws and digging them into a branch. They caught it and pushed it upright again, stamping down the ersatz soil to try to firm it. They got two shots before the director had another bright idea.

'It looks sort of romantic, the two of them like that,' he said. 'Why don't we do February here. Like Valentine's Day, you know.'

'We can't,' someone objected. 'There are leaves on the trees. There aren't any leaves in February.'

'Strip the trees!' the director ordered. I looked around anxiously, but no one seemed to object. I wondered where the Security Guard was, then remembered that he was only here to see that the cats were safe. It was nothing to him if a stall were torn apart, so long as nothing was actually taken away.

'Excuse me,' I interrupted as a couple of minions advanced upon the sapling. 'I don't think you ought to do that. Those trees are only rented. They have to be returned to the Nursery.'

'Who are you?' the director asked coldly.

'I'm the PRO for this Exhibition, and,' I added, with more assurance than I felt, 'the bill for any damage to this Stand will be sent to you.'

We settled down to a short glaring match, which was broken when Dave Prendergast rushed up. 'What's happening?' he asked. 'What's going on here?'

'Absolutely nothing.' Seeing that reinforcements had arrived, the director began a strategic withdrawal. 'We just took a couple of shots. And now—' he turned to his crew—'we'll do August. I always *feel* August as a Jungle Month. We'll take the Big Cats with Lady Purr-fect looking in through the bars at them. And why don't we have one of the other cats in the cage with them? For a contrast in size. Lying between their paws, perhaps?'

With a strangled gasp, Betty Lington caught up Silver Fir and retreated back to her own booth. I must say I agreed with her. No one was entirely happy about the presence of the jungle cats, and that included me. I wondered if I would have accepted their presence as a good idea, had Rose Chesne-Malvern consulted me about it, instead of calling me in after the whole fait had been accompli-ed.

'I'd like to thank you, Doug,' Dave Prendergast said earnestly. 'I heard you as I was coming along the aisle. You kept them from wrecking my Stand. You're a real pal—'

'Forget it,' I said. 'It was a pleasure.'

'If there's ever anything I can do for—'

But I had stopped paying attention. There was more dirty work afoot over by the Big Cage and, Dave notwithstanding, I was beginning to be sorry I had stepped in. At least, while they were busy stripping the leaves off trees, they couldn't be doing anything worse. Right now, they were going up and down the aisles, trying to persuade one of the owners to allow a cat to be posed in the Big Cage. Not surprisingly, they weren't having any luck.

There was only one cat in that aisle who was without someone to speak up for her. Just in case, I began moving towards the director and his crew again.

'Aaraarah.' I recognized the little voice and pushed my way through the crowd. Pandora, looking worried, was being carried toward the Big Cage by one of the crew.

'Oh, no, you don't!' I leaped forward and snatched her away from him. One of us was snarling, and it wasn't Pandora.

'You, again!' The director rolled his eyes heavenwards. '*Now*, what's the matter? Is it your cat?'

'No,' I said, 'but I'm responsible for this Show, and these cats. You aren't putting *her* in that cage.'

'Don't be absurd,' he said. 'Didn't you read the book? Those cats are tame. It's perfectly safe.'

'Right! Then *you* get in the cage with them,' I snarled.

'What is going on here?' Rose Chesne-Malvern's high, clear voice cut through the hubbub. 'What are you doing with my cat?'

'I'm putting her back in her pen,' I said. Leaving no time to argue, I turned and marched back down the aisle with Pandora. Rose Chesne-Malvern came with us. The director, perhaps sensing the weakest link in our chain, followed us.

As I returned Pandora to her pen, he spoke to Rose Chesne-Malvern. 'We only wanted to put the little cat in with the big ones—just for a couple of minutes. There was no danger, and,' he added craftily, 'we'd see that you got double the fee.'

Something flickered in her eyes. I knew that, if the rest of us hadn't been surrounding her, registering varying degrees of horror and indignation, she would have succumbed to the lure.

'Monstrous!' Marcus Opal muttered.

'They can triple the fee,' Betty Lington said. 'Silver Fir won't do it.'

'I'm sorry,' Rose Chesne-Malvern weighed in reluctantly with the majority. 'I'm afraid I can't allow that.'

'It's totally unnecessary,' Kellington Dasczo said. 'They can perfectly well take two shots and superimpose them. *Anyone* knows that.'

'It's not the same,' the director said venomously. '*Anyone* ought to know that.'

I noticed that, across the aisle, Helena Keswick was looking decidedly worried. I went over to her. 'Is anything wrong?'

'I don't know,' she said slowly. 'All this seemed like quite a good idea when Rose first broached it, but now I'm not sure these Perfection people know what they're doing.'

They knew, they just didn't care. But I couldn't comfort her with that thought. 'They seem reasonable enough,' I said. 'At least they'll accept a firm veto. They can't force you into anything.'

'I suppose not.' She was still dubious. 'But I hope they don't want any trick poses of Mother Brown and the kittens. I won't have them frightened or upset.' She glanced at the pen, where Mother Brown sprawled, surrounded by rollicking kittens, twitching her tail for them to play with. 'Really, Rose should have made more inquiries before she got us all into this.'

The Perfection Hosiery crew had withdrawn to Lady Purr-fect's stall for a consultation. Rose Chesne-Malvern had come over to us in time to hear Helena's last remark.

'Are you questioning my judgment?' The two women stared at each other across the railing of the booth. I almost expected to hear a yowling challenge to a cat fight. It had been a long time since I had seen two women so openly dislike each other. They usually try to put a veneer of civility over their feelings—particularly in front of witnesses.

'You *have* been known to have been wrong,' Helena said softly. 'On certain occasions.'

Mother Brown gave an abrupt mewl of distress from the pen and Helena turned to her quickly. It was nothing serious, even I could see that. It was just that the kittens were not wholly aware that they had grown sharp needle-like teeth which could cause pain. Helena took Mother Brown out of the pen, cradling her in her arms, and soothed her gently.

Eyes narrowed dangerously, Rose Chesne-Malvern studied Helena Keswick's back for a moment. If she'd had a knife in her hand, I wouldn't have taken any bets on Helena's continued survival. As it was, she contented herself with the show of umbrage traditional to the affronted Englishwoman.

'Well!' she said explosively, and marched away.

I watched her huff down the aisle and pause at Pandora's cage. She appeared to be doing something there. Casually, I strolled in that direction, hoping she was doing something to improve Pandora's morale. Any fool could see that the poor little beast was nervous and needed some reassurance.

She moved away from the cage before I reached it. Pandora was at the bars, staring wistfully after the retreating back. I saw something new had been added. A sign was attached to the cage. It read, 'Please Do Not Touch The Exhibit.'

The Exhibit moved forward as I approached and rubbed her head invitingly against the bars. Glaring after the fast-disappearing Rose Chesne-Malvern, I defiantly scratched The Exhibit's head.

At the end of the aisle, Rose Chesne-Malvern faltered and slowed, turning to gaze at the draperies shrouding the Whittington Cat with more warmth and approval than I had ever noticed her expend on any living thing. Whether it was because the statue behind the draperies was by Hugo, or whether it was because it was of 18-carat gold, I couldn't say—and wouldn't like to guess.

Then she frowned abruptly, as though recalling herself to duty, wheeled about and marched firmly on her way. Which reminded me that *I* had work to do. Automatically, I latched the door of Pandora's cage. The Exhibit blinked at me in complacent amusement.

'Be a sport,' I said. 'Stay put, like a normal animal. I've got to go shower and shave. I won't be long.'

Suddenly, I *heard* myself—carrying on a conversation with a cat. I glanced about me guiltily before I remembered where I was. None of *these* nuts would think there was anything at all unusual in that. It was

the rule, rather than the exception. Without even
trying, I tuned in to conversations up and down the
aisle.

'Pretty girl,' Betty Lington was crooning. 'Her's the
prettiest girl in the Show, and she has a new contract, and she'll get liver for din-dins . . .'

My eyes met Pandora's and we exchanged a mutual glance of revulsion. But it was hardly any better
directly across the aisle.

'You can lick any cat in the place,' Kellington was
assuring his moody tom, 'with three paws tied behind your back. And you wouldn't stoop to bothering with any of these tabbies—nothing but a pack of
overbred snobs. Just like perfumed, brainless debu-
tantes.'

That one amused us. But Pandora's ears flicked
and her tail twitched uneasily, as another fragment
drifted to us.

'Eat it up, my Precious. For Daddy's sake. It's good
for you. You must eat . . .' Precious Black Jade laid
back his ears and snarled.

'Look,' I said, 'this is all very fascinating, but I
must go. You just relax and—'

Suddenly, a great challenging roar sounded from
the cage at the head of the aisle. Either Pyramus or
Thisbe was feeling his or her oats. I'd like to see
Pearlie King tangle with one of those, I thought, even
without three paws tied behind him. Then I changed
my mind. I wouldn't like to see it. I wouldn't like to
see it at all.

But, once again, I noticed that the jungle cats had
performed their usual trick—they had stopped the
show. There was a moment of utter silence in the
hall. The eyes of both owners and pets had turned
towards the big cage, with varying degrees of wari-
ness.

Pandora, I was glad to see, was the first to recover
from the spell. She flicked her ears, blinked her eyes,

then settled down on her haunches and seemed prepared to snatch a cat nap.

'Good girl,' I told her. 'I'll be seeing you.' She closed her eyes, and didn't bother to answer.

Outside, there was a fine drizzling mist. As usual, the few taxis were either engaged, or driven by men too busy brooding over their own problems to spare a thought for a rapidly dampening pedestrian. I walked along the front of the Exhibition Hall wing of the hotel, thinking I might trap one when it stopped for the lights. After all, it was a technique that worked for hold-up men.

Scanning the street as I walked along, I nearly tripped over the sprawling object on the pavement. A pair of beat-up wellingtons were protecting the lower legs from the rain, the stuffed torso was propped up against the building, as were the kids, trying to keep well back from the weather.

'Penny for the Guy, mister?' one of the kids said, as I stopped to stare. 'Penny for the Cat-Guy?'

I pulled out a handful of change and glanced through it, while they eyed me hopefully. 'That's a pretty good idea.' I nodded to their Guy. 'In keeping with the Show, too.'

'He's supposed to be.' They glowed with pride, anxious to let me know it hadn't happened by accident.

'Very good.' It was, too. They'd done an unmistakable Puss-in-Boots. The usual old jeans and tattered sweater sufficed for the body, but the head was a stroke of genius. A black fake-fur cushion had been resewn, so that the corners became ears, and someone—probably the little girl—had embroidered slanting yellow eyes, and pink nose and mouth. Broom straws stuck out for whiskers.

Of course, some mother was shortly going to be missing her black acrilan-fur throw cushion, and there might be some short sharp demands for an explanation when they returned home. But, right now, they were happy and contented.

That was more than I could say. The more I looked at the dummy cat, the uneasier I felt. There was something . . . reminiscent about it. Something about that black, furry face . . .

Ah, the hell with it! I shrugged off the mood. After last night, I could truly say I had been eating, drinking and sleeping cats for the past twenty-four hours. It was no wonder the sight of even a stuffed one was making my nerves quiver. It was still a very good Guy—somewhere at the back of my mind, the idea lurked that I might be able to do something with it. A couple of Press photos, perhaps. Or, possibly, invite the kids to take up a stand in the Hall itself, to add more colour to the scene.

The kids were still waiting hopefully. No point explaining to them that my reflexes were slowed by a bad night. I pulled out a couple of tenpence pieces and gave them to the kid nearest me. What the hell, I could put it on the Expense Account.

Just then, as though to prove the Lord loveth a cheerful giver, an empty taxi pulled up at the lights. I dived into it while the kids were still shouting thanks after me for my largesse.

Chapter

5

The *office-flat* near the top of the building in Villiers Street was deserted when I reached it. I was just as pleased. Gerry is apt to be a bit too buoyant and talkative in the morning. I just wanted a bit of silence and the opportunity to clear my mind of cats and cat-lovers.

I made a good start with a hot shower. The place ran to a few such luxuries now, thanks to a generous—and, I might say, well-earned—bonus from our last job. I had shaved, dressed, and was browsing through a moderately well-stocked cupboard trying to decide what I fancied for breakfast when the telephone rang.

Like a trusting fool, I ambled over and answered it. Some people never learn.

'Hello, Doug?' The urgency in the voice alerted me. I wasn't going to like what followed.

'Douglas Perkins, here,' I admitted, waiting for the bad news.

'Thank heavens! Look, Doug, it's Dave Prendergast here—'

I felt an immediate rush of guilt. He'd discovered I'd filched that trial packet of Pussy No-Poo. Maybe the Agency had them counted and he had to account for every one. He must have gone looking in every earth tray, until he found it in Pandora's.

'I'm glad you called, Dave,' I said hastily. 'I meant

to leave you a note, but I hadn't anything to write on—you know how it is. I'm afraid I owe you the price of a trial size packet—'

'Stop clowning, Doug,' he said, 'this is serious. You'd better get back here to the Exhibition fast.'

'What's the matter?' Already, I was beginning to know that I'd soon wish it *had* been the pilfering he was worried about.

'That Security Guard,' he said. 'They've found him. The ambulance has just taken him away.'

'Ambulance?'

'Concussion, they think it is. They found him underneath those iron spiral stairs leading up to the Press Gallery. He must have fallen, maybe landed on his head, or hit it on the way down. There's no telling how long he was lying there. He didn't look too good. You'd better get back here right away. The Press are arriving, too. And the Chesne-Malvern bitch has blood in her eye.'

'Thanks, Dave,' I said. 'I'll grab a taxi and come right now, And, Dave—thanks again.'

'Forget it,' he said. 'Anything for a pal.'

We hung up simultaneously, and I dived for the door. My luck was in and I caught a taxi cruising up from Charing Cross Underground, on its way to try for a fare at the Main Line station. He was mollified when I gave him my destination. It was far enough away to be worth his while, after all.

He set me down outside the Exhibition Hall. Anxious though I was to get inside and face the worst, a stray breeze blew the aromas from a mobile hamburger stand across my path and a sudden convulsion from my stomach reminded me that it had been a long time since it had entertained any food—fourteen hours, at least.

I detoured just long enough to collect a hamburger and took a bite of it, intending to finish it inside. One bite—that's all.

Munching that mouthful, savouring it fully, I

strolled into the Exhibition Hall and down the centre aisle where the Special Exhibits (I already thought of them as *my* cats) were installed.

The Perfection Hosiery crew seemed to have disappeared. I noticed Helena Keswick sitting calmly in the corner of her booth and it seemed only courtesy to halt and pay my respects to Mother Brown again.

'Everything all right?' I hailed Helena Keswick.

'Just fine.' She rose and came towards me. 'They've taken all the shots they wanted of Mother Brown and the kittens—without taking them out of their pen. It was silly of me to worry, I suppose, but things seemed to be getting out of hand earlier.'

'Great!' I leaned forward, both hands resting on the stall railing, to peer at the group in the miniature Empire bed. 'I'm glad everything went well—'

Mother Brown raised her head, nostrils twitching. She turned her head questingly, and zeroed in on the scent. She rose abruptly, tumbling protesting kittens in all directions, and stalked over to us.

'Hello, my beauty,' I said, 'how are *you*—?'

A claw descended, hooking into the back of my hand.

'Don't move,' Helena Keswick said quickly. 'She doesn't mean to hurt you. Cats don't often scratch people. People scratch themselves. A cat's claws are curved at the ends, so that they hook into their quarry. You scratch yourself when you pull away—the *cat* doesn't scratch *you*. Just don't struggle, and she'll let go in a few seconds.'

I froze. I had no choice but to take her word for it. Mother Brown glanced up at me quickly, sensing she had won without a fight. She brought her other front paw up and hooked the hamburger out of the bun in my nerveless grasp. Picking it up in her teeth, she retracted her claws, and backed with it to the far corner of her stall, giving me a chummy growl that dared me to come after her and try to retrieve it.

'I wouldn't dream of it,' I told her. 'Ladies first.

Motherhood must be served—and all that sort of thing.'

Helena Keswick watched us both with amusement. Mother Brown paused and raked a bit of fried onion off the hamburger.

'I'm sorry,' I said. 'I'd have told them to hold the onion, if I'd known. Is the ketchup all right?'

Helena Keswick laughed out loud. I began to feel that the hamburger might be considered an investment in good will—as well as being eligible for the Expense Account. 'You wouldn't,' I offered it to her, 'care for a slightly used bun, would you?'

'It's amazing,' she chortled. 'I can't believe it didn't happen by accident, but Rose Chesne-Malvern actually got the right PRO for this Exhibition.'

But an accident-prone Security Guard. To put the best possible light on it.

It didn't seem a good thing to say to Helena Keswick, however. She'd been under a strain, worrying about Mother Brown and her brood. She had a right to some light relief. I bowed to her and continued on my way. There was just one more stop I had to make before I began worrying about the two-legged characters.

I might as well not have bothered. Although she had been watching my approach, Pandora wasn't speaking to me. She made that quite clear, turning her back as I came up to our—*her*—stall.

'Look,' I said, 'I couldn't help it. You saw her. She just waltzed up and snatched it away from me. I ask you, what could I *do*?'

Turning her head only slightly, she damned me for a faithless wretch, unworthy of the devotion of a poor, honest, trusting cat.

'Look,' I said desperately, leaning on the rail, 'just tell me—what could I do? Did you expect me to belt her one, or something? Haven't you any regard for the sanctity of the home and motherhood, and all that?'

She uncurled slowly and turned to face me. Un-hurriedly, she sauntered over. I was just relaxing, thinking we were friends again, when she hooked her claws into the back of my hand. Remembering Helena Keswick's advice, I froze.

'Grryah?' she snarled, deliberately pulling her claws the length of my hand and removing several shreds of skin. Then she sauntered back to the farthest corner of her stall and crouched down, back to me, tail curled around her, still muttering impre-cations.

'All right,' I said, licking the back of my hand and trying to avoid Marcus Opal's sympathetic gaze, 'all right, I can take a hint.'

I stormed outside to the hamburger stall again. 'Two,' I ordered, 'forget the bun on one of them.'

But the order was too confusing. While the con-cessionaire attempted to argue it out with me, I became aware of a pair of pleading eyes just above knee level.

'Are you going to eat *two* hamburgers, mister?' she asked. 'All by *yourself*?'

She was nearly as good as Pandora at making me feel a great, hulking, insensitive brute. 'Why, are you hungry?'

'Oh, yes, *please*.' Her eyes glowed with hope, but dimmed as I pulled a handful of change out of my pocket.

'What's the matter?' Belatedly, I remembered that most children are trained never to take money or sweets from strangers. Unless, of course, they're collecting for a Guy.

'If you give us money,' she said, 'Brian won't let us spend it. Because we've got to get into the Show. And we have to pay our fares, too.'

'Fares?' I was momentarily diverted. 'Where do you come from, then?'

'Peckham,' she said.

'Peckham—that's the other side of the city and across the river. You must really want to see this Show.'

'We've got to get in. So we have to save all the money we get. But—' she smiled enchantingly—'if you give us hamburgers, we'll have to eat them. Because you can't save them up.'

'You're right.' The kid's logic was irrefutable. Her arithmetic was pretty good, too. Somehow, the hamburger I'd planned on buying her had been parlayed into three hamburgers.

'Three more hamburgers,' I conceded without a struggle. 'And I suppose you could use three Pepsis, too?'

'Oooh, thank you, mister.' She turned and signalled to her companions. The older boy glowered disapprovingly—I gathered he was Brian and would rather have had the money—but the younger boy came running up to help her carry the loot. I helped load them up, conscious of a glow of virtue. The poor kids were probably starving, and it was nearly noontime.

I was back inside the Exhibition before I realized that I was only carrying one hamburger, and Pandora was waiting for me. I debated whether it was worth continuing to be in the doghouse with her, and decided to put it to her squarely.

'Look,' I said reasonably, 'for reasons too involved to go into, this is all I was able to get. I'm hungry. How about going halves with me?'

Cocking her head to one side, she appeared to consider the proposition. Then, lashing one paw out suddenly, she hooked the meat out from the middle of the bun and carried it into the corner of her cage, leaving me with my half—the empty bun.

'Thanks a lot,' I said bitterly. 'You're a real sport.'

Sneering, she settled down to enjoy her hamburger. The onions didn't seem to bother her at all. In fact, she seemed to enjoy them, too.

I nibbled moodily at the dry bun, but gave up and roamed off to find the litter bin I'd noticed at some earlier point in my travels.

'Psst, Doug.' The hail from behind the shrubbery startled me. Brooding over the injustices of the world, I had nearly forgotten the reason I had come back to the Exhibition unfed. Dave Prendergast, motioning me into his stall, reminded me.

'Doug, am I glad to see you! Listen, have you seen Rose Chesne-Malvern yet?'

'No,' I said, 'only her cat—*she* was in a lousy mood, too.'

'Listen, Doug,' Dave said urgently, 'there's something funny going on. I can't get to the bottom of it, I'm stuck here on the Stand. But you can wander around—'

He was a nice guy, but a bit naïve. It didn't seem to occur to him that I had no interest in getting to the bottom of anything funny. Quite the contrary. I just wanted to ignore it. And make sure the newspapers ignored it, too. I tried to give him a gentle hint.

'The Press are here,' I said. 'We're photographing the Private Opening soon. Just cool it, will you?'

'Oh.' The idea seemed to startle him. 'Sure, Doug, sure. I'm sorry. I just got carried away—'

'Well, don't,' I said. 'It was quite enough to have the Security Guard carried away. We want to soft-pedal that sort of thing. We're concentrating on the nice pretty little moggies, remember?'

'Okay, Doug, sure, but I think I ought to tip you off—' I saw, gloomily, that Dave was going to have no nonsense about bearing a burden alone and privately—'I heard the ambulance men talking. They found the Guard right here, you know, under those stairs. And the intern said he couldn't explain those head injuries at all. He said they couldn't possibly have been incurred by just falling down stairs!' He leaned back and looked at me expectantly.

'Thank you, Dave,' I said. 'I'll bear that in mind. It

will lighten many a dark hour for me. I hope you don't intend to confide that little item to too many. I mean, like not more than one reporter from each newspaper?'

'Oh.' Something in my tone finally got through to him. 'I wouldn't do that, Doug. Honest, I wouldn't. I just thought you ought to know. I mean, if I don't tell you, who ought I to tell?'

Who, indeed? 'Okay, Dave,' I said. 'Just leave it with me, will you?'

'Oh, sure, Doug, that's what I meant. That's all I intended to do. Honest. I can keep my mouth shut.' He shuffled through several boxes of his product anxiously, like a gambler shuffling cards to reassure himself that he hadn't lost his touch.

'Here.' He picked up a couple of large size boxes of Pussy No-Poo and thrust them at me. 'Compliments of the house. No,' as I hesitated, 'I mean it. Take them.'

There was nothing else I could do. 'Well thanks,' I said, recognizing the gesture of amends, rather than fully appreciating it. 'That's kind of you.'

'Think nothing of it.' He began bustling about the Stand, rearranging the display.

It seemed to be my cue to move along. 'See you later.' I glanced at my watch and discovered that the Exhibition was faking its opening in less than an hour. I knew from experience how fast things would move from this point to the Opening. Already, I was aware of the growing crowds surging through the Hall, of the cameramen, of the bright lights and cables snaking along the floor that meant the television cameras were waiting.

I moved back to the Special Exhibits. That was where it was all going to be happening. The concentration of portable lights was brightest around the satin curtains shrouding the gold Whittington Cat.

When Kellington Dasczo stepped forward, made his witty little speech and pulled the cord to part the curtains and display the gold image to the public gaze, the Exhibition would be 'officially' open, although the public wouldn't come in until tomorrow.

Whatever my personal opinion of him, my duty seemed to lie with Kellington Daszco at the moment. I checked in at the booth opposite. Pearlie King was immaculately groomed, smooth short coat gleaming, pearl-button collar glowing against the dark fur.

Kellington was slightly less well-groomed. Not seeming to notice, he was giving a final brushing to Pearlie King's sleek fur.

'Hadn't you better change?' I suggested. 'You're on in twenty minutes.'

'Yes, yes,' he said abstractedly. 'Plenty of time. I just want to get Pearlie King *quite* settled first.'

'This might help.' On impulse, I proffered one of the large boxes of Pussy No-Poo. 'Compliments of Dave Prendergast. It's quite good, really. Pandora likes it.'

After I'd said it, I felt absurd, giving Pandora as a sort of reference for the stuff. But Kellington didn't seem to find anything odd about it.

'Really?' He snatched at the packet eagerly. 'I say, that's most awfully good of you—and what's-his-name. Pearlie *has* been put off a bit by the disgraceful stuff the Committee provided.'

Quite unselfconsciously, he ripped open the packet and poured it into the earth tray. Pearlie King watched with interest and went over to sniff at it as soon as he had finished.

'Ah,' Kellington breathed, 'I do think that's going to do the trick. You *are* kind.' He beamed at me approvingly. 'You know, I've underestimated you. Oh, I always knew you were clever—rather facile, I thought. I never realized you were so sensitive, had so much feeling—I mean, I didn't know you were a *cat* person!'

I bowed wordlessly. It seemed to be his ultimate in compliments. 'So, now you know,' I said, deciding to

trade on whatever new reputation I had established
in his eyes. 'So, now, will you get the hell to your
room and make yourself presentable. You're on in
fifteen minutes.'

'Fifteen minutes!' he squawked. 'Of course, Douglas, of course. Just hold the fort for me, will you,
please?' He snatched up a few essentials and bolted
for his room.

Outside the shrouded stall opposite, the crowd
was growing thicker by the minute. Hot, bright lights
centred on the satin draperies.

Pandora was right next door. I hoped it wasn't
disturbing her too much. Looking over, I found her
uneasy, but fairly relaxed. She was watching me
intently. I realized that she was not going to get too
upset about anything as long as I was in view.

Pearlie King seemed to be all right, so I moved over
to Pandora. 'Easy, pet,' I said, scratching her head.
She purred softly, thrusting her head into my hand.
It seemed we had buried the hatchet.

Hugo Verrier, preened to the nth degree, appeared
in the next-door stall. Rose Chesne-Malvern, looking
rather the peahen to his peacock, stood beside him.
A few cameras flashed.

Then Kellington Dasczo dashed down the aisle,
looking at his watch. I glanced at my own. 12.30 on
the button. Why had I worried? Kellington Dasczo,
whatever anyone might think of him, was professional to his fingertips.

He took up his stance in front of the curtained
statue. He bowed to Rose Chesne-Malvern, he mentioned Hugo Verrier approvingly, he spoke of each
cat in the Special Exhibits by name, citing a few
salient facts and giving the television cameras time
to pan down the aisle.

He swooped across the aisle and collected Pearlie
King. Holding him close, best profiles turned to the
cameras, he finished the expected, witty, urbane
little speech.

With a flourish, he turned and pulled the cord. The satin draperies parted, the cameras zoomed in for a close-up.

Rose Chesne-Malvern screamed and fainted into Hugo Verrier's nerveless arms. He let her fall to the floor as he stood staring and using a few choice words which should never go out over the co-axial cable, even in this Permissive Society.

Kellington Dasczo stood speechless, but Pearlie King yowled as the arms tightened convulsively around him.

I didn't know whether to curse, faint, or yowl myself, as I stared at the empty pedestal.

The gold Whittington Cat with the emerald eyes was missing. Lost, strayed, or—more probably—stolen.

Chapter

6

I don't even want to remember the next couple of hours. Especially the moment when Rose Chesne-Malvern threatened to sue Perkins & Tate for malpractice.

By the time Gerry (I had hastily telephoned for reinforcements) and I had convinced her that it wasn't a publicity stunt we had thought up, we had to start from the beginning again and try to convince the police of it, too. They took an especially dim view of the fact that I had stayed all night. Gerry came in for his lumps when they found out he had been taking photographs of the golden cat and was the last person, besides the sculptor, to have seen it before the curtains went round it.

'I wish we *had* thought of it,' Gerry said. 'What a publicity stunt! We hit every media of communication—and the Wire Services are humming. Reuters, UP—all of them will be at the Show tomorrow. And Penny's been lining up interviews for all the weeklies and monthlies. If only it was a fake,' he mourned, 'we'd have made PR history.'

I wished we'd done it, too, but for different reasons. It would give me a nice secure feeling to know just where that gold statue was lurking and to be able to produce it when I wanted to. Instead of which, I was sitting around wondering if it had already been melted down, and whether Hugo Verrier really could bring damages against the Exhibition for loss of his irreplaceable work of art.

'You know,' Dave Prendergast said thoughtfully, (we were all having a late lunch in the pub across from the Exhibition Hall, and knocking back our last double before 'Time' was called), 'it seems to me that the police ought to be at the hospital, waiting for that Guard to come round. It stands to reason that he must have seen something. Probably that was why he was hit over the head—so that the thief could get away with the Whittington Cat.'

Gerry and I met each other's eyes and turned to regard Dave without enthusiasm. 'That's an interesting theory,' I said. 'Uh . . . you haven't mentioned it to the police yet, have you?'

'They hardly talked to me,' he said regretfully. 'They were only interested in the people who stayed all night. That's when it must have been stolen, you know.'

'So it would appear,' Gerry said. He looked at me pleadingly. 'Didn't you notice anything at *all*? If we could only—'

'Not a thing,' I said firmly. 'Too bad you can't question the cats. Pandora might be able to tell you something—if she could. She was pretty restless last night.'

'You see,' Dave said excitedly, 'you see! The cats were restless! That proves something was wrong. Do you think I should talk to the police about it? Maybe I ought to go back right now and—'

'They're trying to get some lunch, too,' Gerry said. 'I know it's all fairly urgent to us, but it's only another case of theft to them. It's not like a murder, or some nut hijacking an airliner. I think the police can consider themselves fully justified in having a good lunch and worrying about the case again afterwards.'

'Well, the Guard might have died,' Dave was reluctant to say goodbye to his theory. He brightened. 'He *still* might.'

'In that case,' I said, 'maybe the police *will* go on 24-hour duty. But—' I remembered the saturnine official who had questioned me, and who had clearly felt there were more burning issues at stake in the world than a lot of pampered pets, their idiot owners, and the fate of a statue some imbecile of a sculptor had seen fit to cast in gold. 'I wouldn't really bother them outside office hours unless he *does* die. Even then, I wouldn't push myself too far into it.'

'I don't mean to be *pushy*.' I had chosen the wrong word, and Dave was instantly aggrieved. 'I just thought one had a certain duty as a citizen. After all, they've had signs up on every hoarding saying you should call the police if you think you see anything suspicious.'

They had, indeed. And I wondered how many local stations had cursed the PR boys who had thought of *that* one.

'Sorry, Dave,' I said. 'You're right, of course. But the most suspicious thing I've seen all day has been that camera crew—especially the director. My bets are riding on one of them. They could have whipped the statue into one of their cases—it's only the size of a real-life cat, after all—and transferred it to their van outside without anyone noticing. There were too many of them creating constant distractions for us to have been able to watch them.'

'Yes, but the Security Guard—'

'Might have had a genuine accident,' I said firmly. 'Or he might have tangled with one of the camera crew this morning. Last night probably had nothing to do with it. Now, have another drink, and let the police solve it. That's what we pay rates for.'

'But, listen—' Dave leaned forward, he seemed to have thought of another point.

'Time, gentlemen, please,' the barmaid carolled, turning out a couple more lights.

'I'll take Dave on,' Gerry said, grasping Dave's arm firmly and urging him out of his chair, 'and make good on that drink you promised him. Come on, Dave, there's a nice little club—so new I don't think you'll have heard of it yet—'

It was the perfect bait for an advertising man— they have to be in on the latest. Dave rose eagerly. 'Well, maybe we can talk this over some more—'

'We'll discuss it in depth,' Gerry promised, tipping me the nod. I relaxed, knowing I could safely leave Dave to him.

There was just one other thing. As the last lights went out, I palmed the last chunk of cheese on my plate and slipped it into my pocket.

The Exhibition Hall was dark in the late-afternoon gloom, except for the palely-lit aisle of the Special Exhibits. Again, I felt the unspoken approval as I walked along. 'Here she is, Douglas,' Helena Keswick called to me. We had all slipped over into first name terms, closing ranks against the invading police and reporters.

I halted. Pandora was sitting in the lap of a man who seemed to be visiting Helena. Neither of them appeared to be over-enthusiastic about the arrangement and, seeing me, Pandora gathered herself and took a flying leap, landing on my shoulder.

'Pprrryeh?' She nuzzled my ear. Now that I had come back, it appeared that she was glad to see me.

Marcus Opal looked at us enviously and sketched a wave, as he walked past, heading for the bedroom corridor. As soon as he had gone, Precious Black Jade opened baleful eyes and glared after him resentfully.

Helena's visitor unfolded from the low chair and held out his hand to me. 'Nice to see you again, Mr Perkins,' he said. 'I must say, I didn't expect you to be still here.'

'Perkins & Tate never desert their post when the firing starts,' I said, taking his hand. I recognized him now. Roger Chesne-Malvern, presumably come to stand beside his wife in her hour of trial. Uneasily, I

looked around, ready to disappear if I saw any sign
of her. I'd frankly had as much of Rose Chesne-
Malvern as I could stand in one day.

Pandora rocked unsteadily for a moment, then
settled to her haunches and edged forward, lying
half on my shoulder and half along the back of my
neck. Roger Chesne-Malvern smiled faintly.

'You seem to have made a hit with Pandora,' he
said.

I remembered suddenly. 'Should you be here? I
mean, your allergy. Isn't this the worst place in the
world—?'

'I've been to the doctor,' he said. 'Had a couple of
shots. Been taking them for quite a while now,
actually. Immunizing treatment. With any luck . . .'
he shrugged.

'We're all keeping our fingers crossed for you,'
Helena said warmly. 'This visit—' her eyes met mine
warningly—'is by way of being a test run. Rose
doesn't know he's been taking these treatments.' One
eyebrow twitched upward disparagingly. 'He doesn't
want to raise her hopes too high.'

So Rose Chesne-Malvern wasn't around. I relaxed
and smiled at Roger Chesne-Malvern, although I still
felt a bit awkward about wearing his wife's prize-
winning cat as a neckpiece. 'I hope it works,' I said.
'I mean, it's tough, being allergic, when your wife's
so fond of cats.' I did hope it worked, I'd thought of
the happy ending. 'You could stop boarding Pandora
out then,' I said. 'You could keep her at home with
you.'

'Yes.' Roger Chesne-Malvern smiled oddly. 'Pandora is a nice little cat.'

Helena murmured something to him, and he
turned to answer her. I remembered the chunk of
cheese and fished it out of my pocket, brushing bits
of lint off it, and lifted it shoulder high. 'Fancy a
snack?' I asked.

Greased lightning snapped at my fingers and

flashed to the floor, carrying half the cheese with it. She was a lady—at least, she'd left my fingers. Most of them, and there was still an inch-thick, two-inch-long, wedge of cheese left in them. I looked at it consideringly, wondering whether to let her have it, after that exhibition of greed, or whether to show her who was boss by eating it myself.

Something made me look up and into the stall across the aisle. Precious Black Jade crouched at the bars of his cage, yellow eyes intent on the chunk of cheese in my hand. I remembered that I had heard Marcus Opal beseeching him to eat something at various times during the day, but that he had disdained every tin offered. Maybe he only fancied mousetrap cheese. However, going near Precious could be living dangerously. So could feeding another cat when Pandora was around.

But Pandora was occupied with her cheese, and the way Precious was staring at the remainder couldn't be ignored. At least, not by me. Making sure Pandora wasn't paying any attention, I sauntered over to the stall.

'Okay, sport,' I said—I couldn't bring myself to call him Precious, 'see if this suits your taste.' I poked it hurriedly through the bars at him and retreated back to the Keswick Cattery stall, hoping the beast would eat it. I had the strong impression that Marcus Opal wouldn't take kindly to having anyone else make what he'd consider overtures to his cat.

When I looked back, Precious was in a shadowed corner of his cage, unmistakable jaw movements showing that he was busily disposing of the evidence. I glanced around and saw that my infidelity had not gone unnoticed by Pandora. She crouched at my feet, and I flinched as she sprang.

'Prryeh,' she said, landing on my shoulder and scratching her wet nose on my ear. Evidently I was forgiven. Of course, Precious was a male. Perhaps she was only jealous of other females. Some time, when I was feeling braver, I might test that theory by feeding something to Mother Brown again.

'How about going back in your pen?' I suggested. 'I've still got work to do.'

'Prryeh.' She nestled down comfortably on my shoulder and settled into a steady purr.

Helena and Roger seemed to have forgotten me, but I thought it only polite to say goodbye. Helena smiled cordially, but Roger leaped a mile. It was beginning to get through to me that he didn't really have eyes for anyone else when Helena was around. I wondered what Rose thought of this situation—or whether she had taken enough time out from trailing around after Hugo Verrier to notice that a situation existed at all.

'Before you go, Douglas,' Helena purred, holding something out to me. 'Why don't you borrow this brush until tomorrow. I don't *think*' (which meant she knew damned well) 'Rose has a brush for Pandora.'

Come to think of it, Pandora could do with a nice little brushing—not that she looked at all tatty. It was just that she could look a bit sprucer with a nice gleaming coat. 'Thanks,' I told Helena, meaning it, 'I'd appreciate that. We want to look our best tomorrow.'

Helena smirked at me and it wasn't until I was turning into Pandora's stall that I realized what I had said. We, indeed. This damned place was getting me. I was nearly as crazy as the rest of them. And it wasn't even my cat. Pandora belonged to Rose Chesne-Malvern and, from what I had been seeing here, she represented quite an expensive investment.

I was just starting to brush Pandora when all hell suddenly broke loose at the Big Cage. Pandora, who had been enjoying the attention, dived under the table and hissed.

Up and down the aisle, the others reacted. Kellington Dasczo dropped the book he had been reading

and lurched in front of Pearlie King's pen, spreading
his arms out defensively.

Betty Lington shrieked, and Silver Fir sat up and
blinked. Precious Black Jade snarled softly. Helena
Keswick drew the curtains protectively around
Mother Brown's bed, as though that would shut out
any noise, any danger. Roger Chesne-Malvern
stepped out into the aisle and looked up towards the
source of the disturbance. Only in the end stall was
there no reaction, perhaps because that pampered
advertising agency cat, Lady Purr-fect, was accustomed to eccentric goings-on in her vicinity.

I moved forward to see just what in hell *was*
happening. Marcus Opal cowered against the inside
of the guard rail as both Pyramus and Thisbe raked
outward with their claws, trying earnestly to remove
as much of his flesh as they could manage to reach.
Fortunately, he had succeeded in leaping out of
reach a split second ahead of them. As I watched, he
ducked under the guard rail and scuttled down the
aisle to the safety of his own stall. Behind him, the
frustrated roars of the big cats shook the rafters.

'Really!' Kellington Dasczo said, recovering himself and moving away from Pearlie King's pen. 'I *did*
think everyone here was sophisticated enough *not* to
tease the animals.'

'I'm sorry,' Marcus Opal burbled apologies. 'I just
thought—that is—they looked a bit *lonely*. It seemed
to me . . . a friendly word . . . a pat . . . might
cheer them. *She*,' he spat the word out bitterly,
'hasn't been paying much attention to them all day.'

Which was true, but none of his business. The big
cats, I mean. They belonged to Carlotta, she got along
with them, and they were used to her. It was up to
nobody else to interfere.

Thirty-six hours was beginning to teach me the
difference between the true animal lover and the
sentimentalist. The true animal lover took them on
their own terms, accepted them as individual crea-

tures and—in some strange way—managed to be accepted by them in the same way. It was an alchemy I was aware of, yet hadn't begun to fully understand.

The sentimentalist was dangerous—both to the animal and to himself. Because he interpreted every reaction in human terms. In more than human terms—in terms of wishful thinking. Which was unfair to the animal concerned, and could be downright deadly to the human concerned.

At this moment, I felt vindictively, I wouldn't mind seeing something deadly happen to Marcus Opal. Which was wishful thinking on my part, of course.

'Those monsters should be shot,' Marcus snarled. 'They aren't safe. Rose Chesne-Malvern was insane to allow them into this Exhibition. I don't know what she was thinking of. You mark my words, there'll be trouble from them yet. Bad trouble.'

Since the others were now ignoring him, it seemed only politic on my part to nod. 'Very nasty,' I acknowledged ambiguously, 'very nasty, indeed.'

'Indeed it is.' He pottered over to stand at the dividing rail between our stalls, but I wasn't in the mood to get matey with him.

Pandora crept out from under the table cautiously. I picked her up and went back to brushing her. When I finished, I had better go back to the hamper and see about some dinner for her.

The roars from the end of the aisle were diminishing as, still prowling restlessly, Pyramus and Thisbe accepted that their prey had escaped them.

Chapter

7

The big cats kept prowling restlessly, snarling for the next hour, engendering a malaise that seemed to spread through the Hall. At one time or another, everyone in the aisle glanced nervously up at the Big Cage.

I didn't blame them. I was doing a fair share of glancing myself. Those bars didn't look all that strong to me. And those cats seemed to be growing bigger and uglier, as well as meaner-tempered, every minute.

But Pandora ate her dinner, just the same. Which was more than was happening in the next stall. By now, I was quite accustomed to the running battle between Marcus Opal and his recalcitrant pet at every mealtime. 'Please, Precious . . . nice cat-food . . . yum-yum . . .'

I watched with some complacency as Pandora finished and began polishing her bowl. It struck me that a man could really cut down on his dish-washing time with a cat like that around. When I looked up, Marcus Opal had come over to the dividing rail between the stalls and was watching, too.

'Precious won't eat,' he confided, as though the whole aisle didn't know it by this time. 'He's usually a bit upset at Shows, but he's never been this bad before. It's those animals,' he glared down at

Pyramus and Thisbe (one of them had stopped prowling and was pawing determinedly at the base of the iron bars at the front of the cage), 'they've upset all the cats. And it's so bad for them.'

'Too bad,' I said noncommittally.

'Too bad—it's criminal! Of course—' he glanced back over his shoulder (Precious was snarling softly, crouched in a corner of his cage)—'there is the situation at home, too.'

'Oh?' I was slightly more interested. Marcus Opal had never given any indication that a hotel wasn't his natural habitat.

'Oh, yes,' he leaned forward, even more confidentially, 'Precious has a sweet little queen in kitten to him at home. They're due any moment. Naturally, he wants to be back there with her.'

'Naturally,' I said, doubting that Precious gave much of a damn. 'You must be quite excited about it, yourself.'

'Oh, I am, I am,' he said. 'I can't tell you how excited. It's been the dream of my life: "The Marcus Opal Precious Jewel Cattery". But first, after I retired—the Civil Service, you know—I had to find the right cats. I had Precious Star Sapphire—the queen—for two years, but I couldn't find a really worthy stud. Then, like manna from heaven, I found Precious Black Jade. You can't imagine the excitement I felt.'

'Yes, perhaps I can,' I said. In an odd way, I could. It was too bad he had to find a cat who hated him so much, when he was obviously prepared to expend so much devotion on it. I hoped he had better luck with the one at home.

'Actually,' Marcus said, 'that's why I'm here. The "Precious Jewel Cattery", I mean. I'm looking for another nice little queen for Precious. Perhaps two. Then I can try some crossings with the kittens. I can found the best Manx Cattery off the Isle of Man.'

The early birds among the Exhibitors had arrived

and, having collected their clobber and found their assigned places, were penning their cats for the night. Having done this, they drifted over to the main aisle to look at the Special Exhibits. They were beginning to cluster around Mother Brown's stall, and the coos and cries of admiration were floating over to us.

'I personally think that's disgusting,' Marcus Opal said righteously. 'I would never submit Precious Star Sapphire and her kittens to an ordeal like that. I don't know why Helena Keswick does it. It's a cheap and vulgar playing to the gallery.'

And wasn't the gallery responding! Marcus Opal was green with envy because he hadn't bred his cats in time for the kittens to have arrived and passed the age requirements for an Exhibition Litter. I made a mental bet that any future Exhibition would have the 'Precious Jewel Cattery' heavily represented—very heavily.

Otherwise, things seemed to have settled down to a quiet lull. It occurred to me that this would be a good time to nip back to the office and see if there were any developments there. I could also pick up my razor, pyjamas, and a few things to make to-night's stay more comfortable than last night's had been.

I was just about ready to leave for the Exhibition again, when Penny came in. She began unpacking her carry-all, pulling out a jar of instant coffee, her library book, and two tubes of glue.

'We ran out of glue,' she said. 'There was so much evening coverage to paste into the guard books. And lots of Stop Press in the afternoon editions.'

I tried not to wince. It wasn't exactly the sort of publicity we visualized attracting for our clients. I had to admit, though, that all the names had been spelled right.

'What are you doing here at this hour? You should have gone home.'

'It's only half-past six.' She eyed me hopefully. 'I thought I might be able to come and help you at the Exhibition for a while tonight. I've got everything practically up-to-date here,' she added hastily. 'I can paste up the rest of the stuff in no time.'

She was a good kid, and she didn't ask for much. Other secretaries—even part-time ones—wanted more pay, better hours, time off, and paid holidays. Nobody had explained these things to her yet. Her typing was improving, too.

'All right,' I said, 'don't take your coat off. I was just leaving. Wait a minute—' I had a sudden thought—'I'll be right with you.'

The tin of sardines was still on the pantry shelf. I slipped it into my pocket. It's hard work being photographed, and a hard-working cat deserves an occasional treat. Like a hard-working secretary.

'Come on,' I told Penny. 'We'll pick up a taxi downstairs.' There are advantages in living near a Main Line station.

We arrived back at the Exhibition just as more police were driving up in a couple of cars, all ready for another difficult session of trying to question distracted people among crowds of other people who had been nowhere near the scene of the crime when it happened. You had to admire their persistence.

Penny dashed in ahead—those cats had really got to her—while I was paying off the taxi. I turned to follow her and nearly tripped over them. They had crowded in behind me and were staring up pleadingly.

'Please, mister,' the leader said, 'don't let them send us away, please.'

I was at a loss for a moment, then followed the direction of their worried glances. They actually thought all those policemen had come to chase them away because they were contravening some minor bye-law.

'We aren't making any trouble, honest we aren't,' the other boy said. 'We got a right to be here.' He was a more pugnacious type.

'Please—' the little girl put a grubby little hand on my sleeve and smiled up at me enchantingly—'make them go away again, mister.'

'Look, kids—' I tried to move forward, but they were crowded so close to me that I literally couldn't budge—'don't worry. They aren't interested in you. It's all right, I promise you—'

'Then—' this time, she took a fistful of material and twisted it earnestly, but it was good worsted and the stitches held—'tell them to go away. We don't like policemen. Sometimes they chase kids.'

'Okay.' I patted her head. 'As it's you, I'll speak to them. They won't be able to go away, because they've got business inside, but I'll see that they don't bother you.'

'Thanks, mister, thanks.' I was fleetingly aware of grubby little hands patting me on the back, and then they were gone. Back to their Puss-in-Boots and their plumed collecting hat. I wondered how they were doing. It kept me from wondering why I'd had to play 'big shot' and let them think I could 'fix' the police for them. Why couldn't I have explained properly and made them understand that the police had a theft to worry about and weren't even going to notice them?

But it was too late now. They were watching me surreptitiously as I neared the policeman at the Entrance. I waved to them, then nodded to the policeman.

'Cute little kids,' I said. 'Enterprising of them to make a Puss-in-Boots Guy. We'll be taking some publicity shots of them later. Good human interest stuff.'

'Aaar, probably tealeaves, one and all," he said

gloomily. 'You'd be surprised. You don't know the complaints we get every "Bob a Job" Week.'

Maybe the kids hadn't been so far wrong, at that. 'Oh well, press on regardless,' I said, nodding to him again and going inside.

Penny, as I might have expected, was cooing over Mother Brown's litter. I waved at her as I went past. Pandora woke from what was evidently a light doze as I approached, and rose and stretched, yawning widely.

Just for appearance's sake, I opened the door of her pen, and she strolled out languidly. Not quite ignoring me, she made an exploratory circuit of the stall. I followed her part of the way, then she leaped up on the railing between the stalls.

Blazing, intent yellow eyes followed her progress, but she didn't seem worried. She approached the other pen and she and Precious regarded each other through the wire mesh. There was a low, rapid interchange of growls.

Even then, it didn't strike me as ominous. I was unprepared to see Pandora paw the latch of Precious's cage and let the door swing back. Precious was out of it before I could leap across the stall and stop him. I leaped just the same—there wouldn't be enough left of Pandora to make a pair of fuzzy cuff-links, if she tangled with Precious.

I snatched her up and tossed her on to my shoulder, just as Precious reached the railing. 'Go away,' I snarled at him. 'Get lost! Beat it!'

He approached me warily, ears flattened, belly low. I didn't fancy the idea of being the site of a cat fight, but I prepared to do battle for Pandora's honour.

Incautiously, I put out my hand to shoo him away, and he caught it with his claw. Mindful of Helena Keswick's warning, I froze.

He sniffed at my cuff, then reared up on his hind legs and inhaled heartily all along my sleeve, up to my elbow. I noticed that, somewhere along the way, his claws had disappeared into their sheaths and his ears had flicked up to normal. But his mouth was still open, tip of his tongue curled intently between gleaming fangs as he sniffed around some more.

Then he looked up at me and yowled, urgently, imploringly. I'd never seen an animal trying so hard to communicate something, ask me something. It upset me that I didn't have an idea in the world of what he wanted.

'I'm sorry,' I said. 'I'm most terribly sorry, old chap. I just don't know.'

He yowled again, a wild despairing wail. Pandora jumped down from my shoulder and stood beside him. She stared up at me accusingly, adding her bit to the conversation, but she made it no clearer than he did.

'I'm sorry,' I said again, feeling increasingly helpless in the face of such urgency. 'I don't know.'

This time, Pandora made it clear that she felt I'd let the side down badly. 'All right, I *said* I'm sorry,' I told her.

And then I remembered the sardines in my pocket. They must have smelt them. No wonder they were so annoyed with me for being obtuse.

'Here you are, then.' Feeling a great relief, I pulled out the sardines. It was a rolltop tin with its own key and I had it open in a moment. I set it down in front of them, then was afraid I might have precipitated that cat fight I'd been trying to avoid.

I needn't have worried. Pandora dipped a paw in and flipped out a sardine. Precious gave half a wail, but hunger won and he lunged forward, sinking his fangs into the tin. They continued to eat that way; Precious, straight from the tin, while Pandora dipped a ladylike paw in and pulled out titbits. She sent me a largely unreadable glance, but I gathered I wasn't quite the hopeless idiot she had at first thought—although there was still room for improvement.

'Precious, you're eating!' Marcus Opal had come up behind us. Precious glowered at him and lifted his head out of the tin, as though aware that he was pleasing Marcus Opal by eating and unwilling to continue. But hunger won again and he compromised by lowering his chin into the tin and backing as far away as he could get, dragging the tin with him and growling menacingly all the way.

Pandora watched the tin of sardines slide out of her reach with the unworried composure of a feline who not only knows where her next meal is coming from, but has zeroed in on a sucker to keep her plied with between-meal snacks. She sprang for my shoulder and settled down there purring, gusts of fish-scented affectionate breath wafted past my nostrils. I decided to slip her something less pungent next time.

'He wouldn't eat for me,' Marcus Opal said accusingly.

'Perhaps he favours sardines,' I suggested, feeling guilty.

'I tried him with sardines yesterday.'

'Perhaps he's worked up an appetite since then.' It was the best I could think of, and I hoped it was good enough. Marcus Opal would be suing me for alienation of affection, if I didn't watch my step.

'Perhaps he *has* settled down.' Opal decided to accept my explanation as a face-saver. 'He ought to have some milk, too, he'll be thirsty. Sardines are salty, you know.' He fussed over to the hamper of supplies and pulled out a Thermos, pouring cool milk into the cat's bowl.

Precious watched him approach, then struck out as Opal bent to place the bowl in front of him. The bowl overturned, showering milk everywhere. I thought Precious looked at the droplets a bit avidly, but decided I'd better not say anything.

Marcus Opal had noticed, too. 'I wonder, Douglas—' he picked up the bowl and handed it to me—'if you'd mind trying to give Precious some milk. He seems to like you.'

'I'll have a go.' I poured some more milk into the bowl, Precious was still glowering. I set it down a safe distance from him and backed away from it. 'Come on, sport,' I said. 'You know you're parched—stop fighting it.'

He inched forward slowly, still growling and, with a baleful glare at Marcus Opal, fell upon the milk, splashing it in all directions in the ferocity of his assault.

'You have a way with cats,' Marcus Opal conceded nobly.

I'd been thinking something along those lines myself. Or perhaps that chunk of mousetrap cheese had created a bond between Precious and me. Reinforced, of course, by the sardines. Again, it was a little item I had better not mention to Marcus Opal. I shrugged modestly.

There was an increasing commotion at the next stall, not alone to be explained by the quiet policemen who had been working there since they arrived. Pandora and I strolled across to the dividing rail to see what was going on. After a moment, Marcus Opal abandoned Precious to his milk and joined us.

Hugo Verrier was fighting for admittance to the stall, waving a large black and white glossy photo. I recognized it as one of the ones Gerry had taken the night before the Exhibition opened.

'I have a right to be in here,' Hugo was storming. 'This is my stall. This—' he waved the photo wildly—'is my Work of Art. My stolen Work of Art. Why aren't you police out looking for it, instead of wasting your time here? It isn't here. It's gone! Stolen—you idiots—and you're not even bothering!'

He sounded thoroughly hysterical. I was reminded of Gerry's gloomy comment, when he found out who

Hugo Verrier was—or, rather, who he was related to. 'We might have known there'd be trouble,' Gerry had said, stroking his face reflectively. 'There's bad blood in that family!'

The dark saturnine official who had given me such a bad time yesterday was regarding Hugo with gloomy relish. I had the impression that Hugo was setting himself up for one great big fall. I hoped I'd be there to see it, but it obviously wasn't going to be this time.

Taking a deep breath, the official said, 'We're busy here now, sir. Perhaps you could come back later. We might be able to let you in then.'

'Ridiculous!' Hugo Verrier screamed. 'I insist on my rights. Where's Rose Chesne-Malvern? *She'll* tell you who I am!'

'That's right,' Marcus Opal said softly behind me, 'where *is* Rose? We haven't seen her since that Insurance Investigator asked to speak to her privately—and that was *hours* ago.'

Chapter

8

*U*nobtrusively, *I started searching.* I began in the Press Gallery. There were still a few of the Press around. We were News now, not just Features. I nodded to them, but managed to avoid them. I didn't want anyone else asking me where Rose Chesne-Malvern was. Not until it was a question I could answer.

Through the plate-glass window of the overhanging booth, I studied the movement of traffic on the floor. Penny was at the stall now. Obviously inspired by the example of Kellington Dasczo, who was grooming Pearlie King, she had taken Pandora out of her pen and was brushing her. Pandora seemed quite happy with the procedure. Across the aisle, Betty Lington shook talcum powder into Silver Fir's coat and fluffed it out to an improbable size.

I scanned the other aisles slowly. Quite a few of the long-distance Exhibitors had checked in now and were settling their cats into the pens.

But there was no sign of the trim, self-contained figure we all knew and loathed. A disturbance at the entrance to the Special Exhibits caught my eye. I watched as Carlotta Montera swung down that aisle, pulling a small wagon loaded with red meat.

The roars shook the Press Gallery, directly over the cage, and sent several nervous customers skittering for the safety of the Main Floor. I couldn't see the cage itself, of course, but I had a prime view of Carlotta swaggering down towards it. The roars increased, the nearer she got.

I watched the pattern of traffic change on the floor. Drawn, however reluctantly, by the noise, all those who were in the immediate area moved to the cage. There was quite a crowd by the time Carlotta reached the end of the aisle.

I'd watched this performance from the floor, myself, last night. It was far more impressive from the overhanging balcony. She pushed the wagon under the guard rail and swung over the top of the rail herself, in a flurry of legs and swirling skirt. I saw her lips move as she approached the cage, and the movement of her arms as she slid up the trapdoor. Then she shovelled the first two pieces of meat inside with blurring swiftness. I knew they were being snatched out of her hands as they got within clawswipe of the trapdoor. It was probably too small a door for the animals to squeeze out of, in any case, but I wouldn't have liked to take any firm bets on it.

She pushed the remaining chunks of meat into the cage a bit more slowly, letting the audience gasp and worry about how small the door really was, and whether one of the tigers would force through it before she slid it closed again. The audience loves to scare itself, and has a touching faith that a wild animal would rather chase a piece of raw meat on the hoof—like one of them—instead of settling down to gnaw a chunk neatly delivered to its waiting claws.

With a flourish, Carlotta slid the trapdoor closed. No one quite dared applaud, but the awed murmur was satisfying enough. She swung across the guard rail again and marched down the aisle, the empty wagon rumbling behind her. I knew that she would come back a few minutes later and fill the water pans as though she were taking an encore.

It was a superb piece of showmanship. I only wished she weren't performing it here.

I left the almost-deserted Press Gallery and descended the spiral iron staircase. Very carefully. On impulse, as I reached the ground, I bent to stare into the shadowed area beneath it. But it was empty.

I turned to find Dave Prendergast smiling wanly at me. He looked very seedy—but tractable. It was no time to ask him whether he had seen Rose Chesne-Malvern lately. He had too much imagination to be able to deal with that sort of question.

'Hello, Dave,' I said. 'How's business?'

'Good, Doug, very good. The overnighters are queueing up for the Product, to make pussy's night more comfortable. And we should do a rushing business tomorrow when the rest of them get here. What else can you expect?' His smile widened. 'We're preaching to the converted. As soon as we find out the points that appeal to them most, we'll incorporate them into our television commercials— and we'll be home and dry.'

He might have chosen his words more carefully, but I made allowances for his condition and nodded. Gerry didn't do things by halves. Dave had obviously gone through the afternoon on automatic pilot. But I had every confidence in him. His automatic pilot was probably more efficient than any lesser man's eight cylinders.

'I've been thinking, Doug,' he said.

'Have you?' I tried not to groan. Gerry hadn't used sufficient judgment in choosing the drinks, after all. For Dave, that last one should have been chloral hydrate.

'Quite a lot,' he said earnestly. 'Gerry is right. There isn't any sense in bothering the police with my theory, is there?'

'None at all,' I agreed with relief. Gerry had done his job well, after all.

'I mean, as Gerry said, if they haven't already thought of it themselves, they won't appreciate my pointing it out to them. It might even stop them

getting to the same theory, in the long run, because
they wouldn't like to admit they hadn't thought of it
first, and—'

One of the big cats screamed in challenge, the
other backed it with a tremendous roar. Dave winced
and lifted a slightly shaking hand to his forehead.

'Could you watch the stand for a few minutes,
Doug? I'll be right back.'

I stepped up into the stand and he tottered away.
From my position, I could see the spiral staircase
leading up to the Press Gallery, and most of the Big
Cage. The tigers were in opposite corners, tearing at
their meat. At least, the one in the farther corner was.
The one near to me seemed to be a rather more
delicate eater—perhaps this was Thisbe?

Head tilted to one side, the giant cat gnawed
carefully at the meat, instead of ripping off chunks
the way the other one was doing. I had the sudden
suspicion that Carlotta had not checked to make sure
the meat was completely thawed—a smaller cat,
trying to eat a deep-frozen fillet, would be acting in
just the same way. But there was nothing I could do
about it. I didn't think the big cat would appreciate
my motives if I tried to take it away from her until it
defrosted a bit more.

Dave came back, clutching a glass of fizzing liquid.
'Thanks, Doug.' He sipped at it morosely. 'I think I
can last a while longer now.'

I nodded and slipped away, no more in the mood
for conversation than he was. Rose Chesne-Malvern
hadn't been out of sight for a moment all day, she
must be lurking around somewhere tonight.

Trying to look as though it were just one of my
routine patrols, checking to see that everything was
going smoothly, I began strolling up and down the
aisles, nodding to the Exhibitors penning their cats
for the night.

Some of the Exhibitors had already settled their
cats and left—at least, they'd thought their cats were

settled. Probably the cats would settle when the lights went out, which would be soon now. Meanwhile, they were restless.

Could you blame them? They were pampered pets, admired and petted by everyone who called. Now, suddenly, they had been taken from home, shut up in this pen, and—worst of all—no one was paying enough attention to them. They wouldn't know that the piece of cardboard in the upper corner of the cage read, 'Please Do Not Touch The Exhibit' (although a few crafty ones had clawed it down and were sitting on it). They simply thought they'd lost all their charm, and were going wild. Some of them sulked, most of them paced the front of their pens, calling out brazenly to the passers-by and rubbing the top of their heads against the mesh in an anxious plea for affection.

I strolled along the aisles, whenever possible (that is, when I wasn't being observed), pausing to scratch an ear or head. After all, weren't the cats as much my clients as the Exhibition Committee? My job was to keep up morale when it was flagging.

I was in the Cream and Blue-Cream Longhair aisle, cheering the lot of a lonely little Cream Longhair, when I sensed an angry presence behind me. I turned, carelessly leaving my fingers still thrust through the mesh, absently stroking a nose.

'Well!' she said angrily. She was a short, sharp little creature, ruffled up like an angry hen, and she was looking at me as though she had caught me with a fistful of catnip and an empty sack in my hand.

'It's all right, madam.' I drew away hastily. 'I'm the Public Relations Officer for this Exhibition.'

'And *when* did you last wash your hands?' she demanded.

There must be an answer to that. Besides, they didn't look very dirty to me. I backed a little farther away.

'Oh, I've been watching you,' she went on. 'I've

seen you—petting every cat in the place. Not caring
that you might spread disease from one to the other.
It's a disgrace! If you are the Public Relations Officer,
you ought to be ashamed of yourself. You're setting a
bad example to the Public.'

Her voice was dying away as she opened the cage
and pulled out her cat. When I looked back, she was
brushing its fur. I continued on my way. There had
still been no sign of Rose Chesne-Malvern anywhere.

The last aisle was occupied by some Colourpoints.
They looked like Siamese gone wrong. Perhaps they
were. Long, fluffy coats, with unmistakable Siamese
markings: the dark mask, ears, legs and tail. They
were incongruous, appealing, and thoroughly preoc-
cupied with settling in. It was just as well they were
in the last aisle, they reminded me so strongly of
Pandora, I wanted to get back and see how she was
doing.

And that was where I found Rose Chesne-Malvern.
As white-faced and vindictive as the indignant
owner who had just set upon me, she was berating
poor Penny. Pandora lurked in her cage, watching
with hooded, brooding eyes.

'. . . dare you? My prize exhibit! Who are you,
anyway? What are you doing here?'

'Good evening, Mrs Chesne-Malvern.' For once, I
was the one coming up from behind. 'I see you've
met my secretary.'

'Your secretary?' She was somewhat mollified. 'Is
that who she is? But what is she doing with my—?'

Pandora heard my voice. That deadly accurate
little paw flicked out and disposed of the latch in a
flash. Another flash of fur and she was crouched on
my shoulder, nagging like the rest of them. Somehow, though, it was the best nagging I'd heard all
day. Perhaps because most of the sting was taken
out of it by the way she was rubbing her chin against
my ear.

Rose Chesne-Malvern froze. 'What are you doing to my cat?'

I shrugged. She ought to have been able to see that I wasn't doing anything to her cat. On the other hand, her cat was nuzzling a wet nose behind my ear.

'Come here, Pandora,' Rose Chesne-Malvern ordered crisply.

Pandora continued complaining softly to me. I reached up and patted her reassuringly. I sympathized with her, but there was little I could do. She *was* Rose Chesne-Malvern's property.

The gesture seemed to infuriate Rose Chesne-Malvern. 'Pandora, come down here instantly!' She was a great one for pulling rank, but Pandora continued insubordinate. She had turned to face Rose now, and I could feel one ear flicking restlessly against my cheek, as she continued her jeremiad.

Among the things she was complaining about, I wouldn't be surprised to learn, was that Rose Chesne-Malvern's sharp voice hurt her ears.

'I said, Come Here!' Rose reached up, but Pandora retreated. Rose caught her by one of her hind legs and pulled sharply. 'Come *down*!'

The next few seconds are pretty much of a blur. Pandora hooked her claws into everything hookable and dug in. Rose Chesne-Malvern continued to pull. I heard a nasty tearing sound and hoped it was only my suit.

I tried to be philosophical and reflected that, if my film client ever raised the backing for his projected Pirate picture, I was a cinch for a bit part, wearing a gold earring. One of my ears had just been thoroughly pierced.

Finally, I disentangled myself from them. Rose and Pandora, both breathing heavily and eyeing each other with mutual loathing, had retreated to a corner.

'Come over here, Douglas,' Marcus Opal took my elbow and steered me solicitously into his stall. 'Let

me see those scratches . . . I have a little First Aid
kit here . . .'

He had, too. But I wouldn't have called it a little
one. It was the biggest, most comprehensive one I
had ever seen. Of course, considering the disposition
of his cat, it ought to have been.

He dabbed at my wounds expertly, with various
preparations. He seemed particularly concerned
with my ear, then gave his diagnosis. 'You're very
lucky. That just barely escapes the necessity for
stitches.'

Precious was crouched with his nose against the
mesh of his pen, regarding me speculatively. When
he saw me looking at him, he growled something
softly, interrogatively. That damned cat was still
trying to communicate with me—and I still didn't
know what he was on about. I decided to take it as an
expression of sympathy.

'Thanks,' I said. 'Actually, it only hurts when I
laugh.'

'You *have* won him over,' Marcus Opal said. 'I
wonder—' he hesitated—'if you'd like to give him
his supper. He still won't take anything from me.'

I accepted the tin of cat food and decanted it into
a bowl. Marcus Opal drew back and I pushed the
bowl into the pen. Precious sniffed at it and began
eating slowly, some deep rumblings still coming
from his throat to tell me that he wanted more than
this.

'And *furthermore*,' Rose Chesne-Malvern flung
across the barrier at me, 'I'm staying at the Exhibition
tonight.'

I wondered who had told her that I had been
sleeping in her room, and then I saw Hugo Verrier's
face behind her, grinning maliciously. Gerry was
right, there *was* bad blood in that family.

'That's quite all right, madam,' I said. 'I prefer the
couch in the Press Gallery.' I waited for a guilty start
from one or both of them. At least it should have

wiped that smirk off Hugo Verrier's face, but it didn't.

'Rose,' Hugo said, 'come and have a drink. I want to talk to you.' She didn't seem too pleased.

'And *I* want to talk to *you*,' she said. *That* wiped the smirk off his face.

Before they left, she put some milk into Pandora's pen. Pandora twitched with irritation. I watched, fascinated. I had never seen anything like it before. Her shoulders moved, as though in a shrug, at the same time, her loose skin seemed to ripple upwards and collect in wrinkles just below her neck. It stayed there for a second, then shuddered back into place.

She flicked her ears, then turned her back on the milk, hunching down at the back of her pen, face to the wall, tail tucked tightly along the length of her body. She was a cat who had renounced the world, and milk had no further interest for her.

Rose Chesne-Malvern hesitated a moment, perhaps wondering if Pandora might be starting a hunger strike, under the influence of Precious's example. I was a bit worried about that, myself.

'I'll be back,' she warned me, 'to use my room. And I'll thank you not to go near my cat, in my absence.'

I bowed slightly, consoling myself with one thought. The Committee had hired me, so Rose Chesne-Malvern could not withhold payment in a fit of pique, as she seemed quite capable of doing at this moment.

At least I had the sympathy of the Committee. 'That woman should be shot!' Helena Keswick said bitterly. 'She hasn't an ounce of genuine feeling in her whole body. She can't love anything—she just wants trophies.'

I nodded, unsure of whether she were condemning Rose Chesne-Malvern on my behalf, or on Pandora's.

'Disgraceful!' Marcus Opal said. 'There should be laws preventing people from owning animals unless they really care for them.' He glanced at Precious. 'Care deeply.'

Again I nodded. Betty Lington strolled across the

aisle, carrying Silver Fir. 'Would you like to hold her?' she asked, thrusting the animal at me, as though conferring a consolation prize. I had to take it.

Silver Fir lay flaccid in my arms. One pair of arms was as good as another to her. She lifted her head to a better angle and her empty little eyes scanned the area, as though wondering where the cameras were. I stroked her absently, and a few shimmering white hairs detached themselves and floated languidly on to my dark suit. Unfortunately, one cat wasn't as good as another.

Kellington Dasczo had a more practical solution. Firmly penning Pearlie King, he crossed the aisle too. 'Come and have a drink,' he said. 'It's the only remedy. Drown your sorrows.'

I was in no mood to argue. Handing an indifferent Silver Fir back to her mistress, I went across the road to the pub with Kellington.

When we returned, after 'Time' had been called, Pandora was still turned to the wall.

Kellington patted my arm. 'Try to get some sleep, old man,' he said, rather as one speaking to the recently bereaved. 'It will look better in the morning.'

Morning meant the day of the Exhibition. And then—I'd had enough to be feeling maudlin—I'd never see Pandora again.

In a vicious mood, I charged up the spiral stairs and flung the door open, flooding the Press Gallery with light, hoping to catch them. The room was empty.

From the Gallery, I looked down on the Special Exhibits Aisle. Most stalls were dark now. Only Kellington Dasczo still had a night light going. As I watched, he turned it out and headed for the bedroom corridor. Now the only light was coming from behind the plate-glass window of the Press Gallery. It cast a glare nearly the length of the aisle, probably disturbing the cats trying to sleep.

I had no quarrel with them. I turned the light out and fumbled my way to the couch in darkness.

I slept fitfully, but I slept. I had no idea of the time when the door of the Press Gallery opened. 'Who's there?'

No reply, but I could see the lighter shade of grey where the door stood open against the blackness. There was no darker shadow in the doorway, though.

I lay back, thinking I had not closed the door firmly enough. Beneath me, I could hear faint snarls from Pyramus and Thisbe, belligerent even in slumber. I had nearly drifted back to sleep again, when it leaped on me.

'Aaraarah,' I recognized Pandora's little wail. Frantically, she burrowed towards my chin.

'What the hell—?' She was trembling violently, little mewling cries of distress coming from deep in her throat.

'Easy, easy.' I stroked her, trying to calm her down. 'You shouldn't be here, you know.' I considered taking her downstairs and trying to sneak her back into her cage. Perhaps she caught the thought. Her shivering increased.

'Oh, all right,' I capitulated. 'Stay here—but you'll get me killed.'

However, when the screams woke me in the morning, I found it was Rose Chesne-Malvern who had been killed.

Chapter

9

'Appalling! Appalling!' Marcus Opal paced the length of the aisle and back constantly, wringing his hands. 'Appalling! Can't someone do something?'

'Not until Carlotta comes.' Kellington Dasczo was a pale green around the gills, he tried to keep his back turned to the Big Cage. 'They've called her, she should be here any minute.'

'It's too late, anyway,' Betty Lington said, slightly hoarse from her screaming. 'You can tell that just by looking at her.'

I had been trying to avoid it. Pandora was crouched on my shoulder, still giving an occasional shudder and mewling something from time to time, in the tone of a querulous invalid. I'd tried putting her in her pen when I first came downstairs, but she'd battered herself against the mesh, screaming hysterically, and I'd replaced her on my shoulder. She was there to stay, obviously. I wouldn't have the heart to try putting her in that pen again. And there was no one to object any more.

Rose Chesne-Malvern lay inside the tigers' cage. They had dragged her into a corner of the cage—mercifully, a shadowed corner. We could see that she had been badly mauled, but we couldn't discern the worst details.

One thing was certain, she hadn't crawled into that cage of her own accord. I hoped she had not been conscious at all—or even alive. But it would take an autopsy to determine that now. And the pathologist had better be good at jigsaw puzzles.

'Can't we get her out of that cage?' Marcus Opal asked. 'We can't just leave her there. It—it isn't human.'

The tigers were paying no attention to the body. In any case, they had been well fed earlier. Just the same, I wasn't ready to try to take her away from them. No one else volunteered, either.

'What are we going to do about the Exhibition?' Betty Lington asked. 'We can't cancel it without warning—can we? Can we?' she repeated.

I had been afraid she was looking at me. I checked my watch. It was only seven—the Exhibition opened at ten and would stay open until six. Some of the farthest-flung Exhibitors had come in last night. Others would be well on their way by now, and we had no means of reaching them. We couldn't turn them away at the door, could we? And what about the ones already here? Whatever I said, it was going to be a long day.

'Unless the police decide otherwise,' I said slowly, 'we might as well let the Show go on.'

They nodded agreement. The vote was unanimous. It was what they had wanted to do anyway, they had just been waiting for someone else to voice the suggestion.

'How could this have happened?' Kellington Dasczo moaned. 'We were all here all night.' He looked around. 'Surely, we couldn't *all* have slept through it?'

And that was a thought no one wanted to face. Someone in the bedroom corridor had *not* been sleeping last night.

Someone had slid back the feeding trapdoor of the Big Cage and pushed Rose Chesne-Malvern—dead or unconscious—into the cage. And then? Could anyone have gone back to bed and gone to sleep, knowing what was happening in the Big Cage?

I looked around at them, but they all looked equally dishevelled, sleepless and distraught. I must have looked the same. I caught a few sideways glances and realized that, to this circle, jealousy over a cat represented a perfectly reasonable motive for murder. After the way Rose had pulled Pandora about yesterday, a couple of them might even call it justifiable homicide.

'Can't we at least put a blanket over her?' Marcus Opal was still trying to preserve the decencies in a situation that had left them behind long ago.

'How?' Kellington silenced him.

'Actually, I believe the police never want anything touched at the scene of a crime,' I said. And where were the police, anyway? 'You *have* called the police?'

'I called the RSPCA,' Marcus said.

That was a big help. 'Did you . . . er . . . explain the problem to them?'

'Well, no,' he said regretfully. 'There was no answer. I'd overlooked the hour. It seems incredible that it's still so early.'

I took his meaning. I, too, felt as though I'd lived through a good three weeks since the screams woke me this morning. A *bad* three weeks, rather. And the day hadn't even started yet.

'The police—' I prodded gently.

'Surely that isn't necessary,' Marcus protested. 'I mean, it's appalling enough that this terrible tragedy should have occurred, but to drag the police into it—'

Kellington exchanged a sympathetic glance with me. 'And *how*—' he tried to lead Marcus to the light—'do you think it might have "occurred"?'

'It must have been an accident. She— She—' He floundered, unable, even in his wildest optimism, to think of any plausible reason for Rose Chesne-Malvern to have entered the tigers' cage.

'Precisely,' Kellington said. 'They'll have to know—and they won't appreciate too much delay.'

'It's all right.' Helena Keswick appeared at the back of the group. 'The police are on the way. Roger is going to notify them before he leaves the house. I've just called him.' She looked at us, a bit defensively. 'Well, someone had to.'

'Quite right,' I said, delighted that, for a change, I had been spared one of the nastier chores.

'These beasts should be put down,' Betty Lington said. 'They should be shot—right away. They shouldn't be allowed to live after this!'

'It wasn't exactly their fault,' I pointed out. 'They couldn't help it if someone pushed her into their cage.'

There was a nasty silence. I had blurted out the unfortunate truth. I sensed an immediate drop in my popularity. Except in one quarter.

'There speaks an honest man!' Carlotta Montera strode down the aisle towards us. 'You would penalize my cats because you have used them as a weapon. And you dare to call yourselves cat-lovers!' She glared around at us, sizing us up as prospects for the wrong side of a firing squad.

'That can't be true,' Marcus Opal said. 'We . . . we may not all be angels . . . but none of us would do a thing like that. She must have gone into that cage of her own accord.'

'Why should she do a thing like that?' I honestly wanted to know if he had come up with an explanation yet.

'There are many people,' Carlotta said, consideringly, 'who refuse to believe that there are any cats that will not love them. Mine are one-woman cats—a challenge to such people. But I do not think this Chesne-Malvern was one of them. She did not care enough about cats. Perhaps she did not care enough about anything.'

Certainly, she hadn't cared much about winning friends and influencing people. In the short time I'd known her, I'd noticed the way she rode roughshod over everyone's feelings. It was hard to miss. And, if I disliked her, these people who had known her for so much longer must have disliked her even more. One of them had hated her.

I looked around at them. They seemed pleasant and inoffensive. For the first time, I missed the camera crew—I'd have been delighted to suspect any one of them. But, while I still thought one of them had nicked the golden statue, I couldn't convince myself that one of them could have murdered Rose Chesne-Malvern. For one thing, they had all left the premises while she was still alive. For another, none of them could have had a motive.

I noticed some of them were glaring at me and Pandora. But there were stronger reasons for suspecting other people. I may have fancied Rose Chesne-Malvern's cat, but Helena Keswick had envied her her husband.

'Who has done this?' Carlotta drew the question from all our minds and flung it down in front of us. 'Who has done this?'

Marcus Opal drew back, quivering, as the tawny eyes turned on him like searchlight beams. Then they moved from one person to another. Such was the hypnotic effect of their intensity, it was a wonder we weren't all babbling confessions. I began to see how people could confess to crimes they hadn't committed.

One by one, we moved uneasily under her gaze. Kellington Daszco bumped against me, he moved so hastily. I remembered that he had been the last to leave the Special Exhibits Aisle last night. Had he seen anything? Or had he bumped into Rose Chesne-

Malvern on his way, perhaps quarrelled with her, and—

'Who has done this?' Carlotta gave us one last chance. Nobody rushed to reply.

'No matter.' She shrugged. 'I will find out. I must go now, and make arrangements.' She started down the aisle, paused and turned back to sweep us with that hypnotic glare. '*I will find out!*'

I was very glad that I was innocent. I felt that any murderer would do better to tangle with the tigers than with Carlotta, in this mood.

Roger Chesne-Malvern joined our group just then, looking pale and tight-lipped.

'Roger.' Helena touched his arm gently. 'I *am* sorry.'

He nodded. Together, they went toward the Big Cage. I went with them. In some obscure way, it seemed to be my duty. But as he drew close to the cage, he hesitated and, suddenly, it was an intrusion.

Helena Keswick felt it, too. This time, it was my arm she touched and we both moved away. I looked back over my shoulder and saw that Roger Chesne-Malvern had walked up to the bars of the cage alone and was standing there with his head bowed.

'Have some coffee.' Helena Keswick plugged an electric kettle into a point underneath the table. I sat down in the chair beside Mother Brown's pen. She was playing with her brood, as usual, with a complacent look on her face.

Pandora dropped from my shoulder to the table, looking into the pen with interest. She was quiet now, and not shuddering so much. I thought it might be safe to leave her for an hour or so, while I went back to the office, tidied up, and generally got ready to face a nightmare day. I said as much to Helena Keswick.

'Of course. She'll be all right here.' Helena opened the pen door and popped Pandora inside.

'Are you sure that's all right?' Nervously, I

watched Pandora lifting her feet, trying to avoid the kittens. 'They won't fight, or anything?'

Even as I spoke, Pandora gave a low wail. Mother Brown looked up at her, then rose, shaking off the kittens. She walked up to Pandora and began washing her face. Pandora crouched down, eyes closed, accepting the ministrations. Gradually, her shuddering grew less.

'Isn't that amazing?' I watched bemused.

'Not at all,' Helena said. 'Pandora's still just a kitten herself, she's only eight months old, you know. And they know each other very well. I never dared tell Rose—she was such a martinet . . . about so many things—but I always kept Pandora in the house with my own cats. She was far too young and sensitive to keep penned up alone.'

I felt an irrational rush of gratitude towards her. She was not only an ornament to society, she had a beautiful soul. They don't always go together.

'I often think—' she was still watching the two cats—'that cats are the most telepathic animals alive. They seem to *know* what anyone close to them is thinking and feeling. Oh, I know there are people who say that monkeys are the next step to man on the scale of evolution, but I don't believe it. I think cats are the last trial stage we pass through before we become human.'

Her voice grew wistful. 'And then, when we *are* human, we find we've lost something. Some essential element of communication is lacking—and we have to try to make do with words. We can't just *know*, the way we did before . . .'

The kettle shrieked that it was boiling, and Helena stooped to unplug it. Then she was busy with cups, the jar of instant coffee, milk—the whole rigmarole, and we had stopped communicating too.

The coffee was hot and strong, and the police hadn't arrived before I finished. It seemed like the ideal time to make a break and get back to the office for a while. I

didn't suppose the police would like it, but I can't say I
was duly concerned over their opinion of me. I already
had the feeling that it couldn't get much lower.

But when I rose to leave, Pandora's telepathy
sprang into action again. She leaped away from
Mother Brown's soothing, and hurled herself at the
mesh of the pen, yowling in anguish. I hesitated,
hardly less anguished than she.

'Take her along.' Helena Keswick opened the pen
door and Pandora rushed out. 'She'll be better away
from here for a while.'

'I'll bring her back,' I promised. Helena Keswick
just smiled, a small cat-like smile.

Pandora began to perk up as soon as we entered the
office flat. She leaped from my shoulder (which
settled one problem—I'd been wondering how I
could shave with a quivering cat curled around my
neck) and began an exploratory prowl.

She followed me into the bathroom and watched
for a while, but I failed to hold her attention. The
whole strange new place she found herself in kept
pulling at her and she had to be off to see what else
was around. For the first time, I saw how the
expression 'curious as a cat' had originated.

She seemed happy enough, so I let her get on with
it while I dressed. She was nowhere in sight when I
braced myself and sat down at the desk and reached
for the telephone. This was another reason I wanted
an hour or so away from the Exhibition. I couldn't
neglect my contacts. They often used the PR scraps I
fed them. Now that I had a meat-and-potatoes meal
of genuine front-page news, I had to let them in on it.
The police wouldn't like it, I was sure, but I'd rather
incur their displeasure than that of my contacts. In
the long run, it wouldn't harm me quite so much.

I heard a yell and a yowl from Gerry's room.
Neither sounded too desperate. I picked up the
phone and began dialling.

Gerry charged out of his bedroom, Pandora dangling from one hand. He took a good look at her in the daylight and seemed reassured.

'It's a very nasty feeling,' he said, 'to be awakened by a wet nose shoved into your eye-socket. Someone ought to have taught this cat better manners.'

Pandora spoke sharply and squirmed in his grasp. She seemed to feel he could do with a lesson or two himself.

'Sorry.' He let her drop on to the desk top. She made no effort to get any farther away from him. Shaking her fur back into place, she sat on the desk and regarded him with interest.

'Doug—' he looked at me worriedly—'you didn't nick her from the Exhibition, did you?'

'Relax,' I told him, 'she's only on loan.'

'That's good,' he said. 'She looks like a very expensive bit of fluff to me.' He ought to know, he was the expert on that subject.

I got through to my contact then, and began talking. Gerry sank down on the desk top beside Pandora, listening.

I finished the first call and hung up. He met my eyes and shook his head wordlessly. I started a second call—there was no point in discussing it with him. By the time he'd listened in on a couple more calls, he'd have the whole gory picture.

After a while, he got up and I heard him filling the kettle and opening the cupboard. That took Pandora off the desk in a flying leap. She'd lived in a house—she knew what those sounds meant.

'Oh, all right,' I heard him say, and tins clanked. A peremptory little yowl began giving him orders. Pandora was getting more like herself every minute.

Despite the orders, he brought two cups of coffee in first and set them on the desk. She followed, nagging. The next trip he brought in a tin of shrimps and the tin opener. She jumped up on the desk to supervise while he opened the shrimps.

'One for you—' she took it daintily from his fingertips—'and one for me.' She protested immediately.

'All right, all right,' Gerry said. 'Two for you, and one for me.' He continued hand-feeding her. It was a technique he had perfected across the breakfast table with innumerable birds, and it seemed to work equally well with Pandora.

Footsteps pounded up the stairs and Penny burst into the office. 'Oh, good, you're still here. I—I thought I might be able to help you at the Exhibition again—it's the last day—' She spotted Pandora and swooped on her.

'Ooooh, there you are, my lovely.'

'Don't get too enthusiastic,' I warned. 'She's just visiting.'

'But she's *filthy*. Where have you been, darling?'

Pandora had collected quite a bit of dust somewhere along the way. 'I saw her investigating behind the filing cabinet,' I said, dialling the last number on my Absolute Priority list.

When I looked up, Penny was brushing Pandora down with my clothes brush. Gerry was continuing to offer her shrimps absently, which she continued to accept. I was aware of a strange throbbing noise. After a moment, I traced it to its source. For the first time in ages, Pandora was purring.

The last phone call clued Penny in to the situation, too. Her eyes grew wide. 'Not really,' she said. 'Not eaten by tigers—not *really*.'

'Not eaten, actually,' I said, 'but badly mauled, dismembered.'

'If it happened to anyone,' Gerry said gloomily, 'wouldn't you just know it would *have* to happen to a client of Perkins & Tate (Public Relations) Limited?'

It was a rhetorical question, and neither Penny nor I bothered trying to answer it. Pandora simply kept purring. *Her* world was looking up. Two more slaves were being painlessly broken in. Things hadn't been so good since the old days in Egypt. Certainly, it was a great improvement on life with Rose Chesne-Malvern.

I hated to disillusion her, but it was time to start moving again. 'I'd save those last shrimps for the taxi, if I were you,' I told Gerry. 'It's time we were on our way. *All* of us.' I nodded to Penny. 'This has every earmark of a very hectic day—and it's all hands to the pump.'

Chapter

10

Pandora was interested and unsuspecting most of the way. I had carried her into a delightful new world, and she was willing to go along with me and see what new goodies I could spread out before her. She sat in my lap, looking out of the window with aplomb. Penny had taken possession of the tin of shrimps and, from her spot in the jump seat opposite me, plied Pandora with a tasty morsel from time to time.

It wasn't until the taxi pulled up in front of the Exhibition Hall that she realized where she was. She gave me a long, betrayed look and scrambled up to my shoulder, whimpering softly.

'Easy, doll, easy.' I tried to pat her, but her fur flinched away from my hand, although she remained on my shoulder. It was going to take me a long while to make friends with her again, I knew. Even though she still clung to me, as to a refuge. Still trying to pat her, I climbed out of the taxi, leaving the bill to Gerry. It would all go on the same Expense Account—always provided there was someone to authorize it now.

'He's got a cat!' The cry went up and the kids surged around me, looking up at my shoulder. I thought that they looked vaguely disappointed, but had too many troubles of my own to worry about theirs.

I was not to be spared, however. 'Please, mister—'
they clustered tightly around me again—'please,
mister, we've got the money now, but they won't let
us in. They said kids have got to be accompanied by
an adult. Please, mister, will you be our adult?'

I looked at their grubby, hopeful faces, and I
thought of the police interrogation I was going to
have to face inside. Expecially after disappearing for
so long. My spirit quailed. It was willing—but it
quailed.

'Not right now, kids,' I said. And couldn't stand
the look on their faces.

'Look, I promise you,' I said, 'I'll get you in later.
And you won't have to use any of your own money.
Spend it on lunch.' I winked at the little girl. 'I'll take
you in with me—free—after lunch.'

I dodged away from their effusive thanks then, and
found Penny and Gerry waiting for me at the Entrance. Pandora wailed softly, just once, as we re-
entered the Exhibition.

The last few stragglers among the Exhibitors were
roaming around, carrying their mesh-ended cages,
greeting each other and looking for the pens assigned
to them.

Penny and Gerry walked ahead. They knew the
way, the old familiar routine was waiting for them.
Greet the Press, be helpful and tactful, steer them in
the right direction, and try to play down the sensational elements. (Just try to!) The flashing lights of
exploding flashbulbs lit the horizon like the Aurora
Borealis as we bore down on the Special Exhibits
Aisle. The photographers were shooting the Big Cage
from every possible angle.

All the activity was doing nothing towards calming Pyramus and Thisbe. At least the body was gone
now. Mounds of as-yet-undisturbed sawdust covered
the spot where it had lain.

Carlotta stood in front of the cage, trying to soothe

the animals and respond to the Press at the same time. It was obvious that she wished they would go away and stop disturbing the animals. It was equally obvious that she dared not say so, she was trying to project an image of them as practically household pets.

'See—hush, Thisbe—they are tame, quite safe. Please—remain beyond the barrier. They are upset, nervous but perfectly tame. It is wicked to say—as I have heard people say—that they should be put down because of what has happened. They are not to blame. The one who pushed Mrs Chesne-Malvern into their cage is the one to blame.'

'Are you accusing someone of murder, Señora Montera?' an enterprising reporter called out.

Carlotta hesitated, calculating the alternatives, then straightened defiantly and declaimed. 'It is so! Someone has used my cats as an instrument of death—and I will find out who.'

'Just turn this way, Señora Montera, please,' a photographer shouted. The flashbulbs popped as she turned slowly. I knew him and his rag, and shuddered as I visualized the sort of headline the next edition would carry. 'Tigers, Mistress and Murder' would inevitably loom large in it.

'I will find out,' Carlotta repeated. 'And I will have vengeance!' She had found a Cause as worthy as any Revolution—she was now committed entirely to her cats.

Her attitude made me profoundly uneasy. I wished she would stop threatening the unknown murderer. If she didn't, it was quite possible that she could wind up a victim herself. But I could see that the new revolutionary fervour inflaming her had swept her beyond any such practical considerations. She had a new Cause: her cats—to the barricades—to death—in their defence! She might even kill the murderer first—and that wasn't a comforting thought, either.

Pandora growled softly as I winkled my way through the crowd. Several of the newsmen raised a hand in greeting, but the copy was too good where they were. I knew I'd see them later, after the first excitement had died down and the preliminary stories had been phoned in.

Penny and Gerry had settled in at the Chesne-Malvern stall. The next-door stall appeared to have been surrendered to the police. Blue-coated figures came and went behind the glass of the Press Gallery. I gathered they had commandeered it for this investigation.

Hugo Verrier appeared to have won his point. The deep purple draperies had been replaced by ones of black velvet and one of Gerry's photos of the Whittington Cat (I wondered, in passing, if we could flog some of those photos to the Perfection Hosiery people—they hadn't got any of their own) had been placed atop the sculptor's stand. I thought it a bit odd; but, then, I thought Hugo a bit odd, too. And I hadn't time to worry about it.

Pandora sank her claws into my collar and moaned when I tried to dislodge her, so I left her on my shoulder for a while longer. Penny offered her another shrimp, but that didn't move her either.

I saw burning yellow eyes staring hotly at the tin of shrimps from the cage in the other stall. I relieved Penny of the tin (I didn't want to be responsible for the girl getting maimed) and went over to Precious.

'Care for a bit of brunch, old boy?' He responded so favourably that it seemed safe to unlatch the door of his cage and let him out to eat in comfort. Ignoring the shrimps momentarily, he sniffed my sleeve and rubbed his head against it. Then he stepped back, looked up at me, and began that awful interrogating yowl again.

'I'm sorry.' I felt helpless, stupid, useless. "I don't know. I just don't know what you're trying to tell me. Look.' I tipped the tin out on to the table, shrimps rolled enticingly into a heap in front of him. 'Why don't you just eat instead?'

With a subvocal rumbling that wasn't quite a growl, nor yet a purr, he launched himself into the shrimps. I glanced at Pandora to see how she was taking it, but she was indifferent. She had closed her eyes and withdrawn from it all.

'Oh, Douglas, that is good of you.' Marcus Opal had come back. 'Precious will be quite all right, once I get him home again, but I am glad he's eating. Er—' he hesitated delicately—'you do think the police will allow us to return home tonight?'

He would come up with a cheerful idea like that.

'I'm sure they will,' I said, a bit too heartily, avoiding Gerry's eyes. 'After all, the Show is over tonight.'

It might even be the truth. Perhaps the police preferred to keep murder suspects under fairly close surveillance, but I couldn't imagine that they'd want to retain a hall full of cats in such an enclosed area for very long. 'I expect they'll just take all the names and addresses and ask everyone not to leave the country, or something like that.'

'Yes.' Marcus Opal relaxed. 'Yes, I daresay that would be the most sensible course for them to follow.' He beamed and grew confidential as Precious worked his way through the shrimps.

'You know, there's a dear little Manx tabby for sale over there.' He gestured to the Exhibitor's Pens behind us. 'She's so sweet, and I'm sure she'd breed true—I just feel it. Of course, it will depend on what Precious thinks of her. I'll bring her over and introduce them later—when things have quietened down. See how he takes to her.'

I nodded noncommittally. Marcus Opal was living in a fool's paradise if he thought anything was going to quieten down this afternoon. With less than eight hours before the Exhibitors scattered to their respec-

tive homes, I couldn't see the police easing the
pressure any. Or the journalists.

'Fine,' I said. 'Sounds very promising. Excuse me,
I think I ought to—'

'Oh, Douglas, please!' He caught my arm as I
turned away. 'Before you go—' he gestured towards
the Thermos flask and bowl—'a little milk for
Precious—those shrimps will make him thirsty, and
he won't take it for me. Would you—?'

'Sorry. Of course.' I poured some milk for Precious, who seemed more trouble to Marcus Opal
than he was worth. But perhaps Marcus was the best
judge of that. After all, I knew nothing about the finer
points of cat-flesh—I just knew what I liked.

Pandora was still disinclined to get down. Since
she felt that way, I decided she might as well come
on my rounds with me. It was against the strictest
rules, but in these circumstances, I felt that the rules
had gone by the board long ago. She wasn't going to
bother anyone like this.

She inched a bit closer around my neck as I moved
out into the Exhibition again. I felt guilty for having
brought her back here. Then reminded myself that
there was nothing else I could have done. She wasn't
mine, after all. She had to be returned to her owner.
Who, with Rose Chesne-Malvern presumably lying
in some morgue, must now be Roger Chesne-
Malvern. Who seemed a nice enough fellow (always
provided *he* hadn't murdered his wife), albeit unfortunately allergic to cats.

Our first stop was at Dave Prendergast's stand. He
was hunched in his chair, staring with glassy-eyed
fascination at the commotion around the Big Cage.
He looked as though he hadn't taken his eyes off it
since I'd last seen him. He seemed like the right one
to ask the sixty-four-thousand dollar question.

'How did they get her out of there?'

'God!' He closed his eyes, and shuddered.

I sat down on the edge of the stand while he

recovered, idly running my fingers through a handful of the product, until I remembered what it was. Glancing to make sure his eyes were still closed (admen can get pretty sensitive about these things), I scrubbed my fingers quickly on my handkerchief.

When I looked up, Hugo Verrier was standing over me, glowering at me. 'That's Rose's cat,' he accused.

So long as it wasn't his, I didn't see why he had any cause to act so aggrieved. I said as much, and he paled with fury.

'Just the sort of thing one might expect someone like you to say,' he snarled. 'You—'

'God, it was awful!' Dave opened his eyes, seemingly unaware that he was averting a nasty scene. 'Awful! They earn their money. I'll never listen again when anyone complains all they ever do is give breathalyser tests. God—our police *are* wonderful.' He cocked his head on one side.

'Carlotta wasn't bad, either, come to think of it. She helped. They got poles and they got an iron gate. They pushed the tigers back into one section of the cage—away from the body—then they slid the gate across, making a divided cage. Then, half a dozen on each side, they held that gate in place.

'Carlotta went into the cage with the police and stood beside the gate, talking to the cats, trying to keep them quiet, while they scraped the body on to a stretcher.

'She was the last to leave the cage. As soon as the door shut behind her, they let the gate slide back and those beasts leaped across the cage. They hit the farther side and it moved—*moved*, I tell you! God—' he wiped his forehead—'it was no sight fit to be seen by *anyone*—let alone a poor sod with the mother and father of all hangovers!'

Even Hugo seemed impressed. He sank down on the ledge opposite me, enmity forgotten. 'God!' he echoed.

Pandora moaned in sympathy and tried to crawl

inside my collar. I dissuaded her gently, remembering that, somewhere along the line, she'd seen something even more unfit to be viewed. That must have been when she came streaking up the spiral iron staircase to me.

'She must have been dead.' As though catching my thought, Hugo had gone pale green around the gills. 'No one could have done such a thing if she were still alive.' He avoided looking at the cage. It was easy for him—he had his back to it.

I had too good a view of the Big Cage. A couple of very official-looking gentlemen had joined Carlotta and she was in a smouldering rage.

'They are not dangerous! This atrocity is not theirs. The woman's blood is on the hands of her murderer.'

One of the monsters had come over and was rubbing his head against the bars, for all the world like his miniature domestic brethren in the Exhibition Pens, inviting affection.

'You see?' Carlotta reached up and scratched behind the ear so trustingly presented. A loud throbbing sound could be heard from where we sat.

'You see? Thisbe purrs! What can she understand of human malice? My cats were brutally made an instrument of death. And soon I shall find out who has done this!'

The officials were looking unconvinced, but not so hostile as they had been.

'That woman is a maniac!' Hugo Verrier said. 'She should be locked up for her own good.'

'She's crazy like a fox,' Dave said. 'There's a true-life film in the offing. If the little darlings can play themselves, there'll be another fortune in it for her. Plus the extra she'll pick up acting as Trainer, Technical Adviser, and all that.'

So I'd heard. 'And all this publicity won't harm her at all.' I couldn't help looking at it from a professional angle.

'Practically double her price, I should think.' Dave agreed. 'Who else would want to work with them after this?

'Not only that,' Dave continued, 'but there's been some talk about an appointment to the World Wild Life Commission for her. If she can exonerate those cats—after all this—it should just about clinch that deal.'

I looked at Dave with fresh interest. Gerry and I generally considered that we kept our ears to any available ground—yet neither of us had picked up that particular rumour. If true, it confirmed Dave as someone to be seriously registered for the future.

'So, there's not only the film money at stake,' Dave went on, 'there's all the honour of the appointment— and it would probably mean a foot in the door at getting back into her own country, if she wants to. There's enough wild life there to worry about.'

'You're *all* mad,' Hugo Verrier said. 'Mad—and callous! My God—you're callous!'

Dave and I shrugged at each other. Obviously the lady never had—and never could have—meant as much to us as to Hugo. It occurred to me that, from what I had noticed, he seemed to be taking the whole thing harder than the widower. Still, it was no business of mine.

A great blaze of cheerfulness descended upon me as I realized that this assignment was nearly over. The Exhibition ended officially at six p.m. Give them perhaps another couple of hours to pack all their clobber and be gone—with luck, I could get away and be home by nine. Without luck, I'd still be free of it all by midnight.

Now there was a sliver lining worth contemplating. The clouds—and the police—might hover for a few days longer, clearing up their part of the mess. But I wouldn't have to see any of these characters again—unless I really wanted to. At the moment, with the possible exception of Dave Prendergast, there was no one I ever cared to see again. Most of all, I would be delighted never to have to look at Hugo Verrier's pale green face again.

Something shivered on my shoulder and soft fur rippled around my neck. Pandora. For a few moments, I had forgotten her. She gave a soft plaintive mew, as though she felt something ending too.

My elation vanished. Poor, bloody, forlorn little cat. *Still a kitten herself*, Helena Keswick had said, but already knowing too much of abandonment and neglect. And now she was fool enough to cling to me, while I was already happily planning to slough off the whole Exhibition and all its participants just as fast as possible.

I stood abruptly. Hugo and Dave looked at me in surprise. 'I've got to make my rounds,' I said. 'See that everything is going well—everything else, I mean.'

They nodded and I strode off, Pandora riding on my shoulder like the conscience I abandoned when I first went into public relations work. I walked fast, as though I could outdistance her too.

Judging had started in the Pet Cats Section, and earnest men and women were moving slowly along the aisles, followed by attendants carrying portable tables, plastic bowls of warm water with disinfectant added, and hand towels. Now and again—almost at random, it seemed to me—one of them would stop at a pen and examine the occupant. Then the assistants set down the table, put the bowl on top and waited at the ready with the towel. After examining the cat, the Judge replaced it in the pen and turned to scoop hands through the water and reach for the towel. It was, I understand, like the 'Do Not Touch The Exhibit' signs, for the protection of the cats, to prevent any unnoticed infection from spreading.

The crowds were fairly thick now, and I got caught behind the Judges several times. When I could, I side-stepped; when I couldn't, I stood and watched the judging. I had no idea of the finer points of any of the cats, or just what they were being judged by. Some of the movements of the Judges were mysterious, some were pretty obvious.

That business of running the pencil back and forth across the wire mesh of the cage, for instance, was obviously to make the cat look up—either to check the eye colour, or to test the responses of the cat and see how alert it was. Some of the cats looked up the instant the pencil touched the wire, some leaped for it, some yawned in boredom or didn't bother to look up. I didn't know which attitude got the best marks. Perhaps I was developing into the nervous type, but I preferred the cats who looked up, but didn't dive at you.

If a cat appeared too upset, the Judge didn't try to examine it too closely, but returned it to its pen to come back and try again later. They seemed to have interminable patience—which was more than I had.

Finally, we were in another aisle, the judging behind us, and the Pedigree Shorthairs on either side. Quickly past the Siamese, I needed no reminding. Then a double row of Burmese, the reddish-brown ones somehow all resembling Mother Brown, and even the blue-grey ones having their points of similarity.

The next aisle: the Devon Rex and the Cornish Rex. Strange, friendly, fantasy creatures, with curly astrakhan coats and great butterfly ears.

Abyssinians next—something about them too reminiscent of Pyramus and Thisbe. Odd—perhaps their lynx-like quality reminded one of tigers—I moved quickly away from that aisle, charming though they were.

The British Blue were next. Great, sturdy, steel-blue-furred creatures, with absurd, perfectly round eyes, glowing like fresh-polished copper. I smiled with amusement as I walked down their aisle. Then I stopped smiling.

One pen was empty. Rosettes—First and Second Prizes—were pinned to the bars from bygone Shows. But inside the pen there was just a photograph. A sweet-faced, placid queen, surrounded by a litter of kittens. 'TINTINNABULA,' a hand-lettered sign said, 'died in May. Greatly mourned by her many friends.'

I moved on quickly, grateful that a lump in the throat doesn't show. That was the trouble with them all—they were so sweet, so small, and so vulnerable. Perhaps that could be said of the whole damned human race, too. It didn't bear thinking about—it could break your heart.

The next aisle was an improvement—Manx. Although, inevitably, they brought Marcus Opal to mind. I wandered along, wondering which of the young queens he had earmarked for Precious—she'd have to be pretty tough to hold her own with that roughneck—when I was aware of a presence beside me.

I turned to face a police constable. 'Are you Mr Perkins?' he asked.

'That's right,' I admitted.

'And you were here last night?'

'That's right,' I admitted again.

'Then could you come along, sir? They'd like to speak to you now.'

Chapter

11

I followed the constable up the narrow spiral staircase. As I had expected, it was the dark, saturnine one who was waiting in the Press Gallery.

'Good morning, Inspector,' I greeted him cheerily.

He nodded, stone-faced, giving me no clue as to whether I had demoted him, promoted him, or hit it bang on. (What the hell, I had enough to do trying to remember who was who in Fleet Street, and which way the traffic was flowing. I couldn't take on Scotland Yard too.)

'Good morning, sir. I understand you spent last night here . . . too.'

I sank into the chair he had vaguely indicated with a wave of his hand. I didn't like that opening. It was extremely probable that there wasn't going to be much about this interview that I *would* like.

'That's right,' I croaked, still trying for a cheery, helpful note.

'Yes.' He looked down at a sheet of notes. 'And I presume you saw or heard nothing out of the ordinary . . . again?'

He'd certainly never read anything about how to win friends and influence people—or maybe he just didn't care. 'That's right,' I said, feeling condemned out of my own mouth.

'Yes,' he said again.

'Actually,' I babbled, 'I wasn't down on the floor. I

was sleeping up here last night. I couldn't possibly have heard anything pertinent—or seen anything, either. Just look out of that window. You can't see the Big Cage at all—it's right under the overhanging bit.'

'Yes.' He glanced briefly at the window, as though to reassure himself that it was still in the same position. 'I understand you had a violent quarrel with the deceased yesterday afternoon?'

'No—no!' I protested. 'Not a quarrel. Barely even a disagreement. Just a—a difference of opinion, I suppose.'

'Over a . . . cat,' he said disdainfully. I got the impression that he was a dog man—or perhaps budgies.

Pandora shifted restlessly on my shoulder. I hoped she wouldn't choose this moment to leap down and get chummy with the newcomers. I had the distinct impression that whoever-he-was wouldn't really appreciate the honour.

'Mrs Chesne-Malvern,' I said hurriedly, 'simply felt that she wanted to spend last night with her pet. I had been using her room. She simply let me know that she intended to use it herself last night. That was all. It was all quite amicable.'

Having said which, I immediately wondered how many conflicting and highly lurid stories he had already heard from the others in the Special Exhibits Aisle.

'I see, sir.' His face and voice gave nothing away. 'And so you spent the pertinent hours up here in the Press Gallery?'

'It was the only spare bed,' I said. And then, perhaps explaining too much, I added, 'I—I felt it was my duty, rather. To be on call, in case I was needed.'

'Yes, sir. You're not a veterinary surgeon, are you, sir?'

'No—no, I'm the Public Relations Officer.' I immediately felt the fool he had intended me to feel.

'I see.' He made another note on the sheet in front of him. 'And your rest was not disturbed at all?'

'Well, actually,' I said, 'I did wake up. Once. Pandora—' I gestured toward her—'came bursting through the door and leaped into bed with me. She was shivering violently. She'd been downstairs. She was badly frightened—terrified. She must have seen whatever happened.'

'Yes, sir.' He lifted his head to stare at me. His face, his voice, were dangerously without expression. 'Are you telling me to ask the cat . . . sir?'

Put like that, I saw what he meant, and backtracked hastily. 'Not at all, I just—' I stopped, unsure of what I just wanted to comment on.

'Quite. Did you know the Security Guard?'

'No. No, I never met him.' Dave Prendergast would be glad to hear that they had been thinking along those lines. But it didn't cheer me up any. I was too uncomfortably aware that he had used the past tense. 'I'm sorry about that. I understand he was a nice fellow. When . . . did he die? This morning?'

'Die?' He looked at me oddly. 'What gave you that idea?'

'You—you—er—used the past tense—'

'I see,' he said flatly. 'Sorry. It was a slip of the tongue. I was thinking about the lady's death—not the rules of grammar.'

'No, no, *I'm* sorry,' I said. He hated me. It was written all over him. I was a damned Public School snob who was going to try to teach English to his social inferiors. I considered apologizing further, but abandoned the idea. It wouldn't do any good.

'Then he'll be able to tell you how he came to fall,' I said brightly, hoping to start a fresh hare.

'He can't remember.'

'Not at all? You mean he has amnesia?'

'A simple concussion.' Again his cold grey eyes damned me for a melodramatic imbecile. 'It takes people that way often, sir. He'll remember—but it will take time.'

'Oh, of course. I'm glad— I mean, it's too bad— I mean—' Pandora stirred restlesly on my shoulder again, as though she too thought I wasn't exactly putting my best foot forward and would like to dissociate herself from me.

'Yes, sir.' He lifted his eyes to Pandora and studied her for a minute. 'I understand that's quite a valuable animal?'

'She's a champion,' I said. 'Taken all sorts of medals—and she's still practically a kitten. Only eight months old.'

'Is that so?' He looked at her with more interest. 'There's a lot of mileage in it, then. Good for years and years, I should imagine.'

'At least ten good years,' I hazarded. 'At full steam, that is. After that, she'll probably have to take it a bit easier, but she'll have had a good run.'

'Lots of prize money to be collected over ten years.' He assessed her prospects. 'Then, there's the sale of kittens—she *will* be bred, I presume—?'

'It would be foolish not to,' I said. 'You can't let good championship stock like that go to waste.' I'd been learning something from all my conversations on the Floor.

'And then there's the money to be picked up from endorsements, commercials, that sort of thing.' He too had been doing his homework. 'Properly directed, I'd say there was a small fortune in the animal.'

I began to get uneasy. I didn't like the way he kept calling Pandora 'the animal,' nor did I like all this emphasis on her monetary value. 'Properly directed, yes.'

'Yes,' he said. 'With the right Public Relations, she could go far.'

There we were. He was a budgie man, all right. Probably a bird-watcher, too. People who were cat-lovers would do anything. Killing each other over possession of a cat was, after all, only one step above—or below—cheering their animals on to slaughter Our Feathered Friends.

'Now, see here,' I said. 'I did *not*—'

'A very valuable animal.' He paid no attention to my interruption. 'There was only one other here *more* valuable. Was it insured for much?'

'I don't know if she's insured at all,' I said. 'I've barely met her— I mean, until a week ago—'

'The Whittington Cat,' he snapped. 'Gold, with emerald eyes. How much insurance did it carry?'

'I'm not sure—' I was called to order, and tried to think. (So they were still worried about *that*, were they? Did they consider it part of the same case, or was it two separate investigations?)

'It was a gag,' I said. 'Like insuring some film star's legs, or what have you. I didn't approve, but it was all arranged before Perkins & Tate took over this Exhibition. For the right premium, Lloyds of London or some other insurance company will insure practically anything—especially short-term. The Public doesn't know that it's only for twenty-four hours or so. But they're catching on. It hasn't been used in a long time now. I would have tried to talk them out of it, if I'd known in time. It's pretty corny.'

'Perhaps so, sir.' He gave me the look reserved for imbeciles again. 'However, *this* insurance cover ran for three days, the sum involved is half a million pounds—and Mr Hugo Verrier filed his claim yesterday afternoon.'

I looked at my watch. It was only a quarter past eleven. And it was already one of the longest days of my life. I tried to think of some intelligent comment. Fortunately, he didn't seem to expect one.

'Who does it belong to now?' He shot the question at me suddenly, taking me off guard, as usual.

'Why, er, Hugo Verrier—' (Just in time, I had stopped myself from saying, 'To whoever stole it'—

not the type of answer calculated to endear oneself to
a policeman.) 'That is, possibly to the Insurance
Company now—or as soon as they've paid the
claim.'

'No, sir. Not that cat.' He leaned forward and
levelled his biro at Pandora. '*That* one.'

Pandora rose abruptly, her paw slashed out and
sent the biro clattering to the opposite wall. She
spat softly and violently. Standing there on my
shoulder, she let loose a snarling tirade that gave us
to understand that she was a feline at the end of her
tether. She'd had a terrible night, been frightened
and upset, seen more than any cat ought to see—and
what she *didn't* need at this juncture was some
clown ramming his biro into her face.

The Inspector had snatched his hand back and was
nursing it against his chest, although Pandora had
barely grazed a fingertip. He glared at me, as though
suspecting I was responsible for the whole thing by
means of some sort of remote control.

'That animal is dangerous!' he accused. There was
no difference to him between Pandora and Pyramus
and Thisbe—I could see it in his eyes. He felt she
should be locked up in a cage, too.

'She's upset,' I said. Pandora dropped down into
my lap, still complaining.

The Inspector flinched as she moved. I think he
expected her to leap for his jugular vein. She gave
him a nasty look and turned her back on him,
settling high on my lap, burying her face in the crook
of my arm. I patted her consolingly.

'She ought to go home,' I told him. 'She ought to
have some warm milk, perhaps with a drop or two of
whisky in it, and go to sleep for twenty-four hours or
so. She needs time to get over it all.'

He ground his teeth, almost audibly. 'Precisely
what I was getting at, sir. Where *is* its home?'

Not precisely. He was getting at me—and I knew it.

'Helena Keswick takes care of her,' I said. 'She boards at the Keswick Cattery.'

He still waited, and I admitted it. 'She belongs to Roger Chesne-Malvern now, I suppose.'

'Quite.' He nodded. 'The Chesne-Malverns had—have a Kensington address. They don't keep the animal there with them, then?'

'Mr Chesne-Malvern is allergic to cats,' I said. 'And I understand Mrs Chesne-Malvern thought it was bad discipline for a working cat to be treated like a pet.'

'Quite.' He nodded appreciatively, his face clearing somewhat. I gathered he considered the Chesne-Malvern attitude the first reasonable one he had encountered since this case started.

It was dawning upon me that we had been landed with a fully-fledged aureliophobe in charge of the investigation. Below us, an unearthly yowl came from Pyramus, or perhaps Thisbe. The Inspector flinched again—and I was with him on that one. But it was ridiculous to act as though little Pandora were on the same level as those beasts.

'What *is* happening about that damned statue?' I asked. There was no question of throwing caution to the winds—no matter how cautious I was, he was going to hate me. 'Haven't you found it yet?'

'Investigations are proceeding.' He glared at me. I saw that I was getting under his skin.

'I suppose they've melted it down by this time,' I said pleasantly. 'And Rose Chesne-Malvern's emeralds are probably back in new settings as another pair of earrings.'

'We're doing our best, sir.' At least, he was hating me for myself alone now, and not just because I liked cats.

'As the sign said in the delicatessen, "Our best is none too good," eh?' It occurred to me that, if I kept goading him, he might end the interview in his fury, and let me go. Time was getting on, and I had things to do down on the Floor.

Over his shoulder, through the plate-glass window, I could see crowds eddying down the Exhibition Aisle. We were, I noticed, drawing far bigger crowds than might normally have been expected. The early editions were out now, and the newscasts would be carrying the story. They had rushed over to get double value for their money—not only had there been a large-scale theft here, but now it was the scene of a particularly bloody carnage as well. Value for money, indeed, and the whole family out to enjoy it. No wonder whoever-it-was had said, 'The Public be damned.'

'. . . this morning?' While I was abstractedly counting the house, the Inspector had been asking me another question.

'I beg your pardon?' It didn't improve my standing with him. But then, what would?

'Why did you leave the Exhibition before the police arrived this morning?'

I had been afraid that would come up. 'I wanted to go home—shave, shower, change. Quite natural, you know.'

'Yes, sir.' His tone was carefully neutral. 'And now, tell me, sir—' his voice changed—'why did you take the *cat* along with you?' *Tell me THAT was natural*, his tone implied.

'She was upset,' I said. 'She couldn't be left alone.'

'But there were many people here. The lady from Keswick Cattery it boards with. Mr Chesne-Malvern—it wouldn't have been left alone.'

'They didn't have time to pay attention to her,' I said. 'Not properly. It would have been the same as leaving her alone.'

'I see.' His deep sigh told me that he didn't. That he would never be able to sort out one factor of honest motivation from amongst all us nuts. We were playing some devious game of our own—we must be.

Whoever dreamed of worrying about whether or not a cat were left on its own?

I kept quiet, although he let the silence drag on for an inordinate time. There was no use trying to explain further.

'So you walked out of this Exhibition, carrying an extremely valuable animal, and no one protested?'

'Why should they protest? They approved. Everyone realized that Pandora needed to get away for a bit and calm down.'

He shuddered, looking as though he could do with a bit of calming himself. 'No one watched you leave, then?'

'Of course not. Why should they?'

'What I mean, sir, is—' he had regained control and the unctuous smoothness of his voice should have warned me that a particularly nasty one was coming at me—'if you were not observed when you walked away with the animal, then, in all probability, no one paid any attention when you brought it back.'

'I shouldn't think they did,' I said. 'Why on earth should they?'

'Then—' he closed in triumphantly for the kill— 'how do we know you brought back the same animal you took away?'

I laughed out loud—I couldn't help it. Pandora raised her head and spoke sharply. The Inspector waited, but something in his manner betrayed that he already knew that he had made a fool of himself by asking that question.

'That couldn't be done,' I said. 'Everyone knows Pandora.' He had obviously heard too many stories about ringers being used in horse races.

'You mean,' he said dubiously, 'that an animal is *that* instantly recognizable?' He was going to go down fighting.

'A cat is in this Exhibition,' I assured him. 'You couldn't possibly ring in a double on all these

people. Helena Keswick boards her. The Committee
all know her. Roger Chesne-Malvern would notice at
once—he's only allergic to cats, not indifferent to
them. The idea is absurd. Why—it would be easier to
get away with the Whittington Cat than with one of
the live cats here.'

'Would it, sir?' he asked softly.

'Yes.' I decided the only way to counter was to
look him straight in the eye. 'Yes, it would. But of
course it wasn't done that way, was it? You'd have
solved the whole case yesterday, if it were as easy as
that.' Too late, I remembered that we were involved
in a different case today.

'Perhaps we're not at such a loss as you think, sir.'
He leaned forward and locked glances with me.
Unfortunately, his was inscrutable.

'It wasn't a very subtle crime, you know, sir. It
wasn't subtle at all.'

Chapter

12

They *were changing the* guard at Lady Purr-fect's stall when I got back. Also the cat. Another beautiful, completely anonymous, interchangeable animal. Looking exactly as bored and sulky as the other.

'Is it worth taking her for the last few hours of the Exhibition?' I asked the handler who was tucking the regular cat into the carrying case.

'Have to,' he said shortly. 'This one's needed for a rush photography session. Sits still better, and not so excitable. The other one's too nervy, won't stay still if she can help it. Only good in long shots. Least little thing upsets her and she runs all over the studio.'

'Too bad,' I said. 'She's a pretty little thing.'

He snorted. 'Too overbred. All of them.' His glance flickered at Pandora and up and down the Special Exhibits Aisle. I had the feeling that I'd just encountered another dog man. He snapped the catches on the case and sauntered away.

A couple of acolytes remained with the current Lady Purr-fect, shaking talcum into her fur, fluffing it out, tying the obligatory blue ribbon round her neck. I watched for another moment, then turned away.

It was a relief to see the black, miniature-panther form of Precious slinking towards me. At least he had a genuine personality. It might not be the best one in the world, but it was a definite one.

'Hello, Old Battler,' I said. 'How are you doing?'

The mesh of the cage stopped him, but he was as close to me as he could get. He raised his head and asked me something. Again, the desperate urgency came over loud and clear—but not the question. I began to see how psychologists could devote their lives to trying to communicate with chimpanzees and dolphins. If I had a choice, I'd rather have comprehended that cat than win a fat account which would be absolutely no trouble to Perkins & Tate and pay us a fortune.

'I'm sorry,' I said. I always seem to be apologizing to that cat. If it were happening anywhere but here, I'd feel a complete fool. 'I'm sorry. Give me some clue, can't you?'

'Strange.' Kellington Dasczo had come up behind me. 'Old Marcus treats that cat like a real precious jewel, and yet he's the most miserably unhappy cat I've ever seen.'

'He keeps trying to ask me something,' I said. 'Or tell me something—I don't know which. I wish I could help him.'

'You feel so damned powerless.' Kellington nodded. 'Look at him—he's in perfect physical condition. I'd swear Old Marcus has never raised a hand to him. Mind you,' he added thoughtfully, 'I'd have belted him a few times, if he'd clawed me the way he has Marcus—you've got to show them who's boss, sometimes. Even the best of them. But Marcus has been a saint with that brute, and the only thanks he gets is a sneak attack every time he's off guard. It makes you wonder.'

A long, snarling roar came from the Big Cage. Involuntarily, we both turned to look up that way. One of the tigers clawed frantically at the base of the cage bars, the other paced restlessly behind it.

'Perhaps they're all wild, under the skin,' I said. 'Perhaps some of them can never be tamed, no matter how you try.'

'Perhaps.' He was unconvinced. 'But the beast has never attacked you, has he?'

'No,' I admitted, trying for modesty, 'he seems to like me, rather.'

'Then that proves something in itself,' Kellington said. 'If only we knew what.' He moved forward suddenly and unlatched the door of the pen, stretching his hand inside. Precious backed away, but not too far. Warily, Kellington chucked him under the chin. He offered no resistance.

'You see?' After a moment, Kellington withdrew his hand and relatched the door. 'He likes you. He's indifferent to me. It's only poor Marcus he hates. Why?'

I shook my head. He was right. The theory of primeval wildness couldn't explain it. Otherwise, Precious Black Jade would have attacked one, if not both, of us. But that snarling, murderous fury was reserved for poor inoffensive Marcus alone.

'It doesn't make sense,' I said.

'It must make sense,' Kellington said. 'It's just that we can't interpret it.'

He was right again. Pandora stirred restlessly in my arms, as though aware she was no longer the centre of my attention. I stroked her automatically, still regarding Precious.

Precious inched forward to the door of his pen once more, his molten yellow eyes glaring at me hypnotically. (No wonder the more sensational Sunday papers occasionally ran stories about weak-minded females who had found themselves hypnotized by cats.) I stared into those eyes, and heard the plaintive interrogating yowl again.

'I'm sorry,' I shook my head. 'I can't help you. I just don't know—'

'*Steady* on, old chap.' Kellington shook my arm abruptly, disturbing Pandora, but snapping me out of the spell. 'See here, it's lunchtime. Why don't we nip across to the pub? They do quite a decent lunch

there. Toss Her Majesty into her pen—she'll
survive—and come over with me. You'll feel a lot
better.'

'Yes. Yes, I think you're right,' I agreed. Pandora
would be okay. Gerry and Penny were at the stall,
still using it as temporary headquarters. I started
towards it, but Helena Keswick hailed me.

'How is Pandora?' she asked sympathetically. So
of course I had to pop into her stall and speak to her
for a while.

'Coming along,' I said. 'How's Mother Brown?' It
seemed only courtesy to return the inquiry.

'Just fine.' Helena gestured toward the pen and I
had to step over to have a look.

A tumbled heap of small brown bodies lay in a
mound, shaken occasionally by a seismic shudder
that was a hiccough from one of them. Beside them
sprawled Mother Brown, purring, her eyes blinking
slowly in drowsy contentment.

'Beautiful!' I said, and found I meant it. Helena
smiled her slow cat-like smile.

'Isn't it?' she agreed. Adding, in non-sequitur,
'Pandora should have beautiful kittens, too. Provid-
ing she's bred to the right stud.'

'You said she was still a kitten!' I was instantly
defensive. It was all right for Mother Brown, who
had obviously been born to be a brood cat. But little,
nervous, thoroughly upset Pandora was a different
matter altogether.

'Of course.' The cat-like smile broadened. (I need
look no farther for the Cheshire Cat—here was the
wide, mocking smile which might haunt a man for
the rest of his days.) 'I didn't mean immediately, I
was thinking of the future. The distant future,
perhaps—but the future. They might take after her.
They might be stars, too.'

'Too?' This was a new aspect of Pandora.

'Didn't you know? Poor Pandora,' she said, 'a has-
been so young. She had a part in a television serial,

but it only ran nine weeks. By then, she was at the awkward age—not a kitten, not a cat. I think one of the reasons Rose was so enthusiastic about this Exhibition was because she'd hoped it would be a showcase for Pandora, and help her to stage a comeback. I thought you knew.'

'I must have missed that serial,' I said, not wanting to admit that we hadn't a set. I'd been wondering why Pandora was in the Working Cats Section, but had put it down to sheer nepotism, as her owner was the Organizer.

'Douglas,' Kellington called, 'are you ready?'

I was more than ready. 'Coming,' I answered gratefully. 'Just a minute.'

I turfed Pandora into her pen, but she had no intention of staying there. Giving me a filthy look, she pressed against the mesh of the pen and chirruped seductively at Gerry. He reacted immediately (all his birds have trained him well), recognizing the tone, if not the precise message. It struck me forcibly that the female of the species—any species—is deadlier than the male because she has a better appreciation of her own power. And less scruples about using it.

'What's a nice girl like you doing in a place like this?' Gerry opened the pen and lifted her into his arms. She nestled there smugly, radiating triumph, deliberately not looking at me.

Once you let them know they can work the jealousy racket, you're done for. I turned away, more to show her I didn't care than because the next stall interested me all that much.

Carlotta was just inside the guard rail, talking to Hugo while scanning the Main Aisle with tawny, brooding eyes. I was glad she wasn't looking for me.

'Pure gold?' she repeated Hugo's last words mechanically, not really paying any attention. 'Solid gold?'

'Eighteen-carat—my masterwork,' Hugo mourned,

evidently under the impression that they were reaching a meeting of minds. 'It was destined for a touring Art Exhibition, to go round the world, before being sold at auction in Texas with the rest of the Art. And now it's gone. It was priceless. Irreplaceable.'

Carlotta gestured impatiently, 'Ah, but you had insurance?'

'What is insurance? Mere money. It cannot replace a Work of Art!' He leaned towards her intently, his eyes didn't quite meet hers. They seemed, instead, to be focused on the rubies dangling from her ears.

'But gold,' Carlotta said, 'is not *importante*. It is not bronze, or marble, or—'

'I must work again in gold,' he said. 'Even though I now realize the danger. How much more a hostage to fortune is a Work of Art created in a material of intrinsic value! Yet, I must continue in gold—it's so beautiful, so malleable—it responds so well to one.'

'Least of all—' Carlotta drew herself up portentously, still trying to indoctrinate the reluctant troops—'is it *importante* beside a real cat. The living must take precedence above all imitations.'

Unlikely as it seemed, I found myself in total agreement with her on something. Now that I had seen one of the Exhibition Pens festooned with the decorations won by a lately-departed pet, I understood the full significance of the way Hugo had decorated his stall. The presumption irked me. As though the loss of a well-insured chunk of metal (however valuable) could be comparable with the loss of a warm, affectionate, flesh-and-blood little creature.

'But my golden cat—lost to the world for ever,' Hugo was still mourning. 'Doubtless already melted down in some back room in Bermondsey.'

Carlotta shrugged, setting several gold chains jangling. Hugo assessed them with greedy, gleaming eyes. Even I could see that they'd melt down into quite a sizeable chunk of raw material. But Carlotta was no Rose Chesne-Malvern, to be impressed by talk of Art. Carlotta believed her living cats were Art—and inanimate representations left her cold.

'Your stall is nearest my cats.' Carlotta turned tawny, hypnotic eyes on him. 'Is there anything you have seen or heard to make you suspect who has tried to harm them so?'

Hugo gulped air like a man going down for the third time. He put out his hand, as though to grasp a gold necklet in lieu of a straw, then seemed to become aware that he could not snatch it away from her. Not without a few more preliminaries.

'As a matter of fact,' he said, 'there *is* something. Just hovering at the edge of my mind, but I can't quite get it. Perhaps, if we talked a bit more, I might remember.'

'You *must* remember!' Carlotta commanded. 'So much depends on it.'

'Yes, yes, I'm trying,' Hugo agreed. 'Perhaps if we went somewhere quieter. So that I could concentrate . . .'

It was my personal opinion that Hugo had nothing to remember, but hoped that he might ingratiate himself with Carlotta if he could spend enough time with her. My money was on Carlotta to withstand the blandishments of any con man—even so accomplished a one as Hugo.

If he *did* have any information, of course, he was just the sort to try to sell it at a profit instead of volunteering it to the police. But it was no business of mine—let the Inspector look after his own investigation. Just the same, I looked after them thoughtfully as they left.

'Come along.' Kellington stood outside our stall, with Dave Prendergast.

'Right. You can hold down the fort?' I checked automatically with Gerry. He nodded. 'Do you want us to bring back sandwiches or anything for you?'

'No, you go ahead,' he said. 'I'll take Penny over when you come back.'

The crowd was thinner now. The Press were especially thin on the ground. Having regard to the hour, and the fact that the police had commandeered the Press Gallery with its associated bar, I knew I'd find most of them across the road at the pub.

It was going to be a working lunch. I wondered idly if that were the reason Kellington had decided to attach himself to me.

He wasn't, of course, the only one to want to attach. The kids were waiting close to the Main Entrance, and mobbed me as we emerged.

'Later,' I told them. 'On the way back. I'm just going over to the pub for lunch. Have you lot eaten yet?'

The boys muttered something vague, but the little girl looked up at me and shook her head. 'They won't,' she said. 'They're afraid you'll change your mind.' They glared at her for giving them away.

'Now, see here.' I faced them sternly. 'I promised I'd take you in with me. Free. And I will. So get something to eat for yourselves. After all,' I added craftily, 'it's quite a big Exhibition—and you want to keep your strength up, so that you can see it all, don't you?'

The idea was a new one, and it seemed to jar them. They clustered together for a brief war conference. The words 'fighting fit' floated to me from the huddle. It was the type of remark that an adult doesn't realize—until too late—should have been analysed on the spot.

They broke apart and I knew I had won. 'I'll pick you up here at the Main Entrance in about an hour or so,' I said. They nodded and I saw them heading purposefully for the mobile hamburger stand as we crossed the street to the pub.

The end of the Exhibition had thrown Dave Prendergast into a brooding mood, too. Only Kellington seemed his usual ebullient self.

'I thought your Product went very well,' I tried to cheer Dave. 'Every time I went past your stand, business was booming. The manufacturer ought to be very pleased.'

'Oh, he is,' Dave said. 'He's got his research team working round the clock to get the twin product ready in time for Cruft's. And,' he added gloomily, 'they're talking about putting me in charge of the stand there, too.'

'Sounds fine,' I lied heartily. I couldn't think of a worse fate—but Dave badly needed cheering.

'Oh, it will lead to bigger and better things,' he said.

I agreed. From there, where could you go but up? 'They've got you marked for great things, obviously.'

'I suppose so.' He shuddered. 'But it's the steps along the way that are getting me down. I mean, after the Exhibition closes, I'll have to dismantle the stand—alone.'

I whistled. 'That's going to be quite a job. All those trees and bushes—'

'They're no problem,' he said. 'We never took them out of their bags. The roots are still bound up in balls of earth and covered with burlap. We just slipped them into the stuff as they were. They can be pulled out in nothing flat and sent back to the Nursery. The trouble is the damned product.'

'It *is* a bit thick,' Kellington sympathized.

'Thick—it's two bloody feet deep! And it's got to be shovelled back into sacks and carted back to the factory. I wouldn't mind that so much—' Dave gazed darkly into the middle distance— 'but we left the shovel sticking into the stuff in one corner, so that the Exhibitors could pinch a sample for their earth trays and—'

'What shovel?' I asked. 'I've only seen a pitchfork there.'

'That's just it,' Dave said. 'Some sod stole the shovel. And the pitchfork, too.'

Then I remembered that I hadn't even seen the pitchfork after the camera crew had overrun the stand. But it was too late for that information to be of any use to Dave.

'All I've got left to work with,' Dave brooded, 'is the trowel.'

I nodded. There wasn't much to say. Dave did have a nasty task ahead of him, but it's these little vicissitudes along the road of life that separate the men from the boys.

The waitress brought our steak-and-kidney pies, and Kellington ordered another round of drinks. We tucked into the meal—there was no telling when we'd get our next one. In the ordinary way of things, I felt there was probably a lot more than there seemed to be to closing down an Exhibition. And, with the police around to complicate things, it might be midnight before we finished.

'Considering everything,' Kellington said thoughtfully, 'I think it was a very successful Exhibition. You certainly handled the publicity well.'

I winced. 'Considering everything,' I said. I'd had quite a few vicissitudes along the way on this one, myself.

'Of course, I always handle all my own public relations,' Kellington said. 'But I've been very favourably impressed by the way you've managed this. I certainly intend to recommend Perkins & Tate, if anyone asks my advice about public relations.'

'Thanks a lot,' I said. His recommendation, and five pence, would get us a ride on any bus in Town.

'Yes—' Dave surfaced suddenly—'great work, Doug. You sure got maximum coverage for the Exhibition.'

'Thanks,' I said wryly, knowing he wasn't really paying any attention to what he was saying. He was on automatic pilot again. Otherwise, he would have realized that that was the last compliment he should have paid me.

He made it sound as though all those bright, publicity-attracting items, from grand larceny to murder, had been deliberately engineered as elaborate publicity stunts. All the fun of the fair, with Perkins & Tate (Public Relations) Ltd.

'My round, I believe.' I pushed back my chair and headed for the bar.

Chapter

13

I picked up the kids at the Main Entrance and, true to my word, took them in with me. 'Now look,' I said, as I turned them loose inside, 'if anyone asks you, you're my guests. My name is Doug Perkins, can you remember that?'

They gave me a collective disgusted look. 'Doug Perkins,' they chorused.

'Fine. I'll be over in the Main Aisle. You kids look around and enjoy yourselves. But, remember, I'm trusting you to behave—don't pet the cats, don't get anyone upset, no running or shouting—or out you go. Okay?'

'Okay.' They nodded reassurance to me, and melted away into the thickening crowds. Only the little girl looked back over her shoulder to give me a grateful smile.

I waved to her, then turned to follow Dave and Kellington, automatically scanning the other aisles as I walked past. Everything seemed to be going as well as could be expected.

'Douglas!' A familiar figure hailed from one of the aisles. 'Come here and tell me what you think of this.'

Marcus Opal cradled a little tabby Manx female in his arms. She was almost golden in her markings, with deep topaz eyes.

'Very pretty.' I stroked her, as they both seemed to

expect me to do. She had the fine, silky fur that told
me she was not quite a year old. (Already I had
learned to guess at the age of a cat by the texture of
her fur.) 'Very nice.'

'Yes, she is, isn't she?' He turned her towards me
eagerly. 'Look!' There was a distinct depression at
the base of her spine, even deeper than the usual
obligatory dent. It was somehow decisive, it seemed
to give promise that no kittens of hers would ever be
born with vestigial tails.

'Of course, one can never be sure.' Marcus ran his
index finger into and out of the depression lovingly.
'But it seems a good sign. A very good sign.'

'She's very good stock.' The owner closed in with
the hard sell. 'I've bred her parents four times
now—and there's never been a Stumpie in a litter
yet.'

'Yes, quite a nice little thing.' Marcus was trying to
play it cool, but his arms tightened around the cat.
'It will all depend, of course, on what Precious
thinks of her. If I could take her over and introduce
them . . . slowly. You see . . . Precious is rather
high-strung. I'd like to give him time to get used to
her—then we can tell if it would work out if I bought
her.'

The owner didn't look too happy, but she saw his
point. She looked vaguely familiar—I realized I'd
seen her wandering up and down our aisle several
times, always lingering near Precious's pen. So she
had had her doubts about compatibility too.

'I'm exhibiting other cats,' she said reluctantly,
'so—'

'I'll take her over myself,' Marcus said, 'now. You
can come round later and see how she's doing. I'll
take good care of her, I promise you.'

'I'm sure you will.' She came to a decision. 'If
you'll just take her bowl, and her chopped liver, her
milk, her brush—' Marcus had the cat, so she loaded

me down with the clobber—'she can have the afternoon with your Precious. I'm sure he'll love her.'

I'd read somewhere that, in nature, the male doesn't attack the female. I'd have felt better if I thought Precious had read the same thing. Then I remembered how well he got on with Pandora, so perhaps it was true. I hoped so, because the little cat seemed even more defenceless than Pandora—perhaps because she had no tail. I knew that a tail is of practically no use to a cat in a fight, but the way they lash it around when they're preparing to fight gives the impression that, like kangaroos, they could swing a nasty haymaker across the chops with it if the opportunity arose.

'Of course, I'll have to change her name,' Marcus was musing, as I followed him back to our aisle. 'Precious Amber? Precious Topaz? Precious Canary Diamond?'

'I like Topaz,' I said, juggling her bits and pieces. Over Marcus's shoulder, she blinked her great topaz eyes at me.

I couldn't resist. I fished a chunk of chopped liver out of her dish and fed it to her while we walked along. A few crumbs sifted down on to Marcus's shoulder as she nibbled daintily, but he didn't seem to notice.

That was more than could be said for Pandora. We were just abreast of her pen, and she flung a snarling curse at me.

It was surprising how guilty that cat could make me feel. Nose up against the mesh of her pen, tail lashing, she left me in no doubt about her feelings. Every time she turned round, she caught me two-timing her with another cat! Furthermore—her nose twitched furiously—I had never given her chopped liver!

I was in no position to argue. With a glance of apology to the little Manx, I scooped a dollop of chopped liver out of her bowl and dropped it in front

of Pandora's pen. Then I followed Marcus into his
stall and unloaded the clobber on to his table.

Precious peered out of his pen suspiciously, his
attention about equally divided between me and the
little female. Still firmly entrenched in Marcus's
arms, she looked around with amiable interest.

'How about sharing the wealth?' I asked her. She
was a sweet-natured little cat and seemed undisturbed as she watched me dish some of her chopped
liver into Precious's bowl. 'Courtesy of the little
lady,' I told him, unlatching the door and pushing
the bowl inside.

He asked me his usual question before beginning
to eat. I shook my head, wondering what made him
so different from the usual run of cat. Are some of
them throwbacks to the wild? I might have thought it
a Manx trait, were not the little female nestled
placidly in Marcus's arms, accepting his admiration
as her due, giving every indication that she thought
he was just fine. So it was not that Marcus had
some unfortunate defect, unnoticeable to humans,
which rendered him unacceptable to cats. No, whatever the problem was, it seemed to be peculiar to
Precious.

Marcus was edging closer to the pen, holding the
little female away from him slightly, aware that his
proximity might make Precious take a dislike to her.
Poor Marcus—why he was so fond of that damned
ungrateful cat, none of us would ever be able to
understand.

'Shall I?' I took her from him and set her down in
front of the pen. Precious looked up briefly from his
bowl, then went back to polishing it. Topaz watched
him with calm assurance, a female who was prepared to bide her time, if ever I saw one. She settled
down on the ledge outside the pen and concentrated
on ignoring Precious. I felt she had the situation well
in hand.

It was time to make my peace with Pandora. Gerry

had let her out of her pen so that she could get at the chopped liver, and waved me to keep an eye on her while he and Penny went over to the pub for their late lunch.

She didn't look up as I approached, although I could see that she had finished her sample of chopped liver. 'All right,' I said. 'So I'm a louse. Don't worry, Gerry will remember to bring back something tasty for you. You females have him all broken in.' I stretched out my hand to scratch her head.

She caught me by surprise. Her claws slashed at me, leaving a trail of bleeding welts across the back of my hand. Automatically I lifted it to my mouth to lick away the blood. I hadn't thought she was *that* annoyed with me.

'No, really.' Helena Keswick had been watching, and crossed the aisle to stand beside me. 'You mustn't allow her to get away with that. They're lovely creatures, I know, but if they aren't disciplined occasionally, they'll make your life miserable. You have to show her who's in charge. You're going to have to discipline her.'

'Silver Fir has never been any trouble to me,' Betty Lington said complacently. She had been shaking yet more talcum powder into Silly's fleece (which must have been standing straight out from it all—if the beast ever got caught in the rain, she'd be a plaster statue in three minutes). 'I wouldn't even know *how* to discipline her.'

Well, I was with her part of the way. I raised my tingling hand. I knew how, but I didn't know where. Where *do* you spank a cat?

Pandora bristled, presenting an unfamiliarly fuzzy surface. Her eyes dared me to make a move. But I agreed with Helena—I would, if I could. I made a couple of feints towards the upraised bush of her tail, thick and bushy as a fox's brush. She sneered at me, defying me.

'No, no,' Helena Keswick said sharply, 'not there. Haven't you ever seen a mother cat disciplining her kittens?'

I shook my head. The whole thing was out of my line. Helena was most at home in this territory. From the next stall, I saw Marcus nod to me sympathetically—*he* knew all about vindictive cats.

'The mother cat,' Helena explained kindly, and clearly, 'always aims at the ears. Just lightly—*very* lightly. But it seems to get through to them, as nothing else does. You can forget all about folded newspapers and that sort of thing—it may work with dogs, but not cats.'

She advanced upon Pandora, who backed away slightly, as though recognizing that she was meeting her match. Then Helena's hand flashed out, as quick as Pandora's paw, and flicked Pandora twice across the ears, lightly but firmly.

Pandora retreated, shaking her head. 'Now, you,' Helena turned to me. 'So that she gets the full message. But remember—*lightly.*'

Pandora, still watching Helena, wasn't expecting an attack from my quarter. I felt a swine, but it was a question of survival. 'No,' I said, flicking her other ear with my fingertip. '*Naughty* girl. *Bad* Pandora.'

Helena beamed at me approvingly, as Pandora swore softly. 'Now put her back in her pen,' she directed me.

Hesitantly, I opened the cage and waved Pandora inside. Ears laid back against her head, a nasty look in her eyes, she obeyed, nevertheless. I felt a new sense of power.

'*That's* right,' Helena Keswick approved. 'You've got to show them who's boss—it's for their own good, after all.'

Pandora curled up in a corner of her cage and closed her eyes, as though recent events had had nothing whatever to do with her. I frowned slightly.

'Don't worry,' Helena said. 'She's all right. And she'll be a lot better when she wakes up. You'll see.'

In the next stall, I saw Marcus Opal flex his fingers and swing his hand experimentally. Then he met the molten yellow eyes of Precious and his hand fell back by his side. He smiled placatingly. There was no doubt who was in charge there. Precious had Marcus firmly under his tyrannical paw. It was too bad, but that was the way it was.

'Silver Fir never needed any treatment like that,' Betty Lington said righteously, before returning to her stall across the aisle.

Silver Fir was too stupid ever to let rebellion cross those vacant spaces where other cats lodged a brain. But there was no use telling Betty Lington that. She wasn't, I felt uneasily, all that much brighter herself.

There didn't seem to be much else for me to do at the moment, so I left Pandora sulking and went off on another patrol of the Exhibition.

Everything seemed to be going smoothly. Smiling evasively, I sidled past a group of unsuccessful pet-owners who were having an indignation meeting about the nepotism, favouritism and plain incompetence of the Judges who had failed to award rosettes to their Little Darlings.

Others exhibitors were beginning to pack things back into hampers, already looking forward to the time when they would be leaving for home. The Judges moved about, weary but still cheerful, coming down the home stretch now. A couple more hours and the Exhibition would be officially closed. I wondered how much longer it would take to clear up all the odds and ends, so that we could all go home.

I waved to the kids. They were huddled at the end of one of the aisles, in deep conference about something. Only the little girl noticed me and waved back; but she, too, was deadly serious, intent on whatever fate of the world they were deciding. I was rather relieved. I didn't feel up to childish conversation.

I turned into the Main Aisle again, giving wide berth to the cage with Pyramus and Thisbe. One of them—I had never sorted them out; in terms of colouring, nasty disposition and evil intent, they seemed about the same—was reclining at the back of the cage, growling. The other prowled just behind the bars, now and again raking a claw out through the bars in its winsome way. Carlotta was nowhere to be seen. I wondered what arrangements she had made for shifting her pets; perhaps she was seeing to that now.

Pandora still appeared to be sleeping as I walked past, so I thought I'd drop in and pay my respects to Mother Brown. A faint trace of pipe tobacco cut through the strong sent of cats. Automatically, I glanced back at Hugo Verrier's stall, but it was empty.

Just short of the stall, I saw them. Helena Keswick and Roger Chesne-Malvern, sitting side by side, a cigarette glowing in her hand, a pipe in his. They didn't notice me, they were talking together with that air of intimacy which can seldom be faked—or mistaken.

Abruptly, I turned into the stall before I got to them. Betty Lington looked up at me in pleased surprise. She was dusting Silver Fir with talcum powder again—it appeared to be a kind of occupational therapy for her.

'Look Silver,' she said, 'here's Uncle Douglas come to see you. Isn't that sweet of him?'

She swept the animal into my arms, as though that were the highest accolade she could bestow. Although not expecting it, I managed to catch the cat as it collided with my midriff, a cloud of white powder arising from it as it hit.

Coughing in the smog of talcum, I managed a sickly smile. Limp as an old fur stole, Silver Fir slumped in my arms. Betty Lington beamed on us both. 'We *do* love visitors,' she announced. 'And we were just beginning to feel a *weensy* bit neglected. We haven't seen anyone in hours, except the old police—and one didn't feel that they were *simpatico*.'

'I had that feeling about them myself,' I agreed, and she beamed.

'I wonder if I could ask you a very great favour,' she said. 'Could you look after Silver Fir for me for a few minutes, while I go to the Little Girls' Room?'

'Of course,' I said, 'delighted.' I'd been wondering how I was going to carry on some inane conversation with her, when all I really wanted to do was to think over the implications of the scene in the next booth.

'Oh, thank you.' She dashed away, and I stood there, the limp hank of fur that was Silver Fir in my arms, and glanced casually at the next stall. They were still immersed in conversation, completely unmindful of the world around them.

This, then, was the scene—or close to it—that I had stumbled on that first night in the darkened Press Gallery. Not Rose Chesne-Malvern and Hugo Verrier, as I had assumed, but Helena Keswick and Roger Chesne-Malvern.

No wonder Roger was taking booster shots to try to cure his allergy. With his hay fever, playing with Helena Keswick was playing with fire, indeed. And no wonder Helena had been so pleased with his progress—and so interested in keeping it a secret from Rose.

It was none of my business, of course. Whether it might be the Inspector's business, I wasn't sure. As the subject had never come up in the course of our conversation, I didn't feel it was up to me to mention it to him. Quite probably, it had nothing to do with what had happened. A man can find another woman more agreeable than his wife without feeding that wife to the tigers. Divorce gets easier every day—and it's so much more civilized. Whatever else he was, I had the feeling that Roger Chesne-Malvern was an extremely civilized man.

'Douglas! Douglas!' There was no rest for the weary. Marcus Opal beckoned me across the aisle. Taking a firmer grip on the flaccid Silver Fir, I went over to see what he wanted.

'It's going very well, I think,' Marcus confided jubilantly. 'Precious seems to like her. I feel I ought to go and report to her owner. I was wondering . . . could you take care of her while I'm gone? It will just be a few minutes.'

'Of course,' I said, then was aware of Pandora stirring in the next stall. 'If I could just . . . ?'

'Naturally, naturally,' Marcus followed me into the stall and, as I sat down beside the pen, dumped little Topaz into my lap. Those extravagant topaz eyes blinked up at me trustingly as she settled down on my knees. Silver Fir was a dead weight in my arms.

Pandora came to the door of the pen and regarded me consideringly, as Marcus bustled off. 'Now, look,' I said, 'I can explain everything—I've been framed.'

'Prryah?' That talented little paw snaked out and unlatched the door before I could move, immobilized as I was by furry bodies.

She marched out of the pen and brooded at us all for a minute. To my relief, she seemed to accept my story. She jumped for my shoulder. That was her domain. So long as no other feline had usurped that spot, I was going to get the benefit of the doubt.

'Good girl,' I said. 'That's my lovely sweetheart.'

A throat was cleared judiciously at the entrance to the stall. I looked up to find the Inspector—or whatever he was—watching me with his usual lack of expression. Which, as usual, did little towards masking his real thoughts.

There I was, a cat in my lap, one in my arms, and one on my shoulder, reeking of fragrant talcum powder, and baby-talking the beasts. It confirmed every worst suspicion he had had of me.

'Just one question, sir,' he said, managing to make the 'sir' itself sound like a question. 'Have you seen Verrier lately?'

Chapter

14

'Verrier?' There was a blank moment, while I tried to adjust my thoughts. 'Hugo Verrier?'

'Yes, sir,' he said flatly. 'Verrier.'

Verrier. My thoughts raced out of control now. Not Hugo Verrier, not Mr Verrier, but Verrier. The suspected? The accused? The convicted? At what point in the judicial process does the impersonalization set in?

The Inspector seemed to realize that he had given just a bit too much away. 'We want him to help us with our inquiries,' he said, smiling falsely as he used the other damning cliché. 'Just a formality, sir.'

'Of course,' I agreed glibly. 'As it happens, I haven't seen Verrier for hours. I was talking to him this morning, but I haven't seen him since.'

'Was that before you decided to go home?' The nasty note was back in his voice.

'Actually, it was after I came back.' (You don't get far in Public Relations if you can't blandly ignore implied criticism.)

'And you haven't seen him since?'

'That's right.'

He stood there indecisively, but frowning to try to make it look as though he were considering which of several highly important moves he should make next. (I recognized the technique—he could do well in PR if he ever left the Yard.)

A couple of Exhibition Hall carpenters came up.
'All right to start taking this down, mate?' one of
them asked me. 'Not the whole thing—just the guard
rail, like. Give us an 'ead start when you lot clear out
tonight.'

I checked my watch and nodded, 'Okay.' It was
unlikely that we would be busy enough to require a
guard rail for the remaining hour. Most of the activity
on the Floor now was created by the Exhibitors,
milling back and forth, exchanging addresses and
gossip. The public had been drifting away for some
time, responding to the inner clock which warned
them of approaching tea-time.

The carpenters moved into Hugo's stall and began
dismantling the guard rail. The photograph on the
draped sculptor's stand looked oddly unprotected as
the first rail fell away.

'Just one more thing, sir.' The Inspector turned
back to me. 'You won't be rushing away immediately
the Exhibition closes, will you?' It was an order,
tactfully phrased or not.

'I hadn't planned to,' I said defensively.

'Quite.' He glanced down the aisle. 'And you'll tell
the others, will you, sir? It will be less conspicuous
if you go round. We'll want to speak to all the Special
Exhibitors in this aisle again, after the Exhibition
closes.'

'I'll tell them,' I said. This time, he went away.

'Fraternizing with the law, eh?' I could see that
Gerry had had a very working lunch. He leaned
against the shaking guard rail and leered at me.
'Think it will get you time off for good behaviour?'

Penny giggled as the guard rail swayed forward
and back again in slow motion. Gerry took a determined grip on it, obviously thinking he was the one
swaying. The cats and I watched with interest.

'Perhaps I shouldn't have had that last one.' The
rail curved forward again, swooping Gerry nose-

to-nose with little Topaz. She blinked at him amicably.

'That's a very pretty puss.' Gerry swung back to standing, still trying for nonchalance. 'Do we know her?'

'She's his lady-friend.' I gestured towards Precious. 'Or she will be, as soon as they've been properly introduced.'

Gerry looked at Precious, crouched up against the bars of his pen, glaring out at us, and recoiled. 'My God—they can't send a kit up in a crate like that! It's murder!'

'Here we are!' Betty Lington rushed up and swept Silver Fir out of my unresisting grasp. 'Say thank you to Uncle Douglas,' she instructed her. Silver Fir looked through me vacantly.

As Betty Lington bore Silver Fir off, the guard rail gave way with a tearing crack. Penny, standing directly behind him, braced her hands against Gerry's back and kept him from toppling backwards. Topaz took off from my lap and flew for refuge to the top of Precious's cage. Precious transferred his attention from outwards to upwards.

Still holding a section of the guard rail, Gerry stared at it blankly. 'Don't know my own strength,' he muttered.

'Ta, mate, I'll 'ave that.' One of the carpenters came up and whipped the railing out of Gerry's hands. Then they went to work on the railing dividing the stalls. Gerry watched them, his face clearing.

'Had me worried for a minute,' he admitted. 'Since I seem to be fit, after all, is there anything to be done?'

'You might go up and down the aisle and spread the happy news,' I said. 'We are formally requested not to leave when the Exhibition closes. The police require further assistance with their inquiries.'

Gerry whistled softly. But the carpenters were advancing on the railing at Marcus Opal's stall, and

I had visions of Topaz taking off for regions unknown. 'Sorry,' I said, 'we can talk about it later, I'm
rather fully occupied cat-sitting right now.'

Sure enough, Topaz was preparing to spring when
I pounced on her. 'Steady, baby. Easy, now, easy.'
After a restless moment, she settled down in my
arms again.

Pandora, undisturbed by the carpentry, had spread
out along my neck and shoulder. Fortunately, she
seemed prepared to overlook Topaz—so long as I
wasn't feeding choice titbits to her.

'I think,' Penny said wistfully, 'I'll go over and say
goodbye to Mother Brown—if that's all right with
you.'

'Sure it is,' I said, 'run along. And take your time.
There's nothing urgent to be done here.'

She hurried across the aisle and Helena Keswick
smiled warmly in welcome. Roger Chesne-Malvern
wasn't there now. I wondered where he had gone. I
ought to be thinking about handing Pandora over to
him soon. Or perhaps to Helena.

Or perhaps—a low, mean, unworthy thought
sneaked into my mind and took root rapidly—
perhaps those immunizing treatments were failing
and that was why he had disappeared again. To
nurse his allergy in the open air. Perhaps he
wouldn't even want Pandora now.

The carpenters were getting into the swing of it.
That railing was demolished already and they
moved on to the Lady Purr-fect stall. As usual, her
attendants seemed to be elsewhere. I could see white
fluff where she pressed against the bars of her cage.
The carpenters paused and looked in.

'There now,' one of them said, 'that's what I call a
proper cat. Pretty, like. Not like some of them 'orrors
some of 'em are so keen on, wiv funny dirty faces an'
bits missing.'

I was swept by a wave of irrational fury. How
anyone could prefer a chocolate-box cat with no

personality—I pulled myself together. It was nothing to me.

Dave Prendergast came up to me, carrying a new shovel. 'Have you heard the news?' he asked. 'The guard is coming out of it. That means he'll be able to identify his assailant. He's given the police a description already.'

'Actually,' I said, 'I *have* noticed that things seem to be moving. By the way, I don't know if it pertains to you, but the police have asked everyone in the Special Exhibits Section to remain after the closing.'

'Oh, *thanks*,' Dave said. 'I'll stay. They must mean me, too. My stand is only just around the corner. I'm sure they'll want to see me, too. Besides, it will be hours before I'm all cleared up and able to leave.'

Translated, he wouldn't have missed the coming hours for the world. His eagerness would have flattered the Inspector.

'Oh, well, duty calls!' He shouldered the shovel and moved off. I watched him swing away to his stand with renewed zest, only wishing that I could think of some way to skip out on the proceedings.

I was still looking after Dave, when I saw Marcus returning from that direction. The kids were trailing along some distance behind him and I gave them a cheery wave. Then, the first cold shudder congealed in a pellet at the base of my neck and rolled down my spine.

Those kids weren't casually drifting along in the same general direction as Marcus Opal—they were deliberately *stalking* him.

Marcus returned my wave happily, thinking it was for him. 'Good of you, Douglas—' he bustled up— 'very good of you. All's fairly well settled. She's moving her other exhibits out to her van. Then she'll join us for the acid test—not that there's much doubt.' He glanced towards the cage fondly. 'He's interested. He's definitely interested.'

Marcus reached out to take Topaz from my arms.

The rest is a bit blurred. Precious let out an unearthly yowl from his cage. The kids converged on us like a swarm of battling demons. 'There he is!' one of them shouted.

Whirling dervishes, they swirled past us to Precious's cage. On the way past, they battered Marcus Opal. I collected a few thumps, too—just for good measure.

'No! No!' Marcus dashed over to try to pull them away from the cage. He was outnumbered, as well as being outclassed. The strength of each one was as the strength of ten because they hated his guts. I'd never seen such fury as glowered from their eyes—except . . . except for the way Precious glowered at him.

Despite Marcus, they wrenched the cage open and hauled Precious out of it. There was a flurry of fur and kids, shouts and frantic yowls. You had to be quick of eye to sort out the mêlée and see that what looked like a determined effort to pull the cat apart was being abetted by an equally determined effort by the cat to hurl himself into all three pairs of arms at once.

The other Exhibitors in the Main Aisle hurried over. Helena Keswick and Kellington Dasczo plunged into the brawl and rashly tried to sort out the participants. Penny had come over with Helena, but stood irresolute. Betty Lington stood by, holding Silver Fir, both of them watching with the same smug look on their faces. Such a thing, they seemed to imply, could not happen in a really well-run Exhibition.

Being rather overloaded with cats myself, I couldn't do much to help. Or perhaps that was my excuse and my real paralysis was caused by the fact that there was a curious doubt in my mind as to just which side I ought to be on. (The determined scrawl chalked on the outside wall came back to me: 'CHAMP IS OURS'.)

There hadn't been many blessings for me to count during the course of this Exhibition, but I was grateful for one. At least the Exhibition was over. I had been aware for some time of the successive dimming of lights in the subsidiary aisles as the Exhibitors packed up and went away. The rest of the Exhibition Hall must be nearly deserted now, the Main Aisle was the last pool of bright light. We were having our final little scandal in comparative privacy.

'Now, what is going on here?' Helena had managed to pull the smaller boy away. Kellington had opted for the easy way out and was controlling the little girl.

The kids and Marcus all spoke at once. 'He's MY cat!'

'There appears to be a certain unanimity of opinion on the subject.' Gerry wandered over with Dave Prendergast, who was now clutching a pitchfork. 'Can anyone elucidate?'

The kids looked at him blankly. 'What makes you think it's your cat?' Gerry translated.

'Its is ours.' The smaller boy flung out an accusing finger at Marcus. 'He stole him last year. We saw him do it, but he got away in his car.'

'Nonsense,' Marcus Opal said. 'Why should I do a thing like that? Precious is mine. I bought him.'

'His name's Champ,' the boy said, just as Gerry said, 'Then you'll have the bill of sale, of course.'

'Of course,' Marcus agreed. 'Naturally I don't carry it around with me. At home . . . somewhere among my records . . .'

'That's a lie,' the older boy said. 'Make him show it to you, mister. He can't do it.'

'Can you prove the cat is yours?' Kellington asked. 'Can you identify it?'

'Sure we can,' the boy said. 'Ours is the only cat around without any tail at all. He lost it in an accident. Our uncle told us when he gave him to us.'

Champ fell off a lorry, and his tail snapped right off.'

'No, it didn't,' the other boy said. 'He lost it in a fight. Another cat bit it off. Our Champ is the best fighter in the whole city.'

That, I believed. The kids were in deadly earnest. It was too bad they hadn't their facts straight. Marcus Opal was twitching with glee.

'You see?' he crowed. 'You see? They don't know anything about that cat. They don't even know there is such a breed as the Manx. How could they possibly have owned one?'

It was a good point, but hardly decisive. I wondered if Marcus had been such an expert on cats when he was the age these kids were. The others seemed to be having second thoughts along the same lines.

Helena loosened her hold on the boy. Kellington let go of the little girl and she sidled closer to me. Something was lacking in Marcus's passionate claim of ownership. He wasn't getting any co-operation from Precious. He seemed to realize this suddenly.

'Make him let go of Precious!' His voice was rising unpleasantly. 'Look at him—he's strangling Precious. Precious can't breathe. He's dying!'

If Precious couldn't take care of himself, it was the first time he'd been in that condition since any of us had met him. We looked at the boy and the cat. The kid had a stranglehold on Precious, all right, but Precious didn't seem discomforted by it. Although his head was twisted to one side, and one paw was caught awkwardly under his chin, he wasn't even trying to struggle.

'Give me that cat!' Marcus advanced on the kid, who backed away. Precious's eyes narrowed to slits, he growled and lashed out with all three available paws. But not at the kid—at Marcus.

'What are you doing in here?' Marcus shifted his attack. 'Children aren't supposed to be running around unaccompanied. How did you get in here?'

'We *came* in.' The little girl spoke up, for the first time. She pressed closer to me, laying her hand on my sleeve possessively. 'We're guests—we're guests of Mr Perkins.'

And it all clicked together in my mind, as her hand tightened on my sleeve. The embroidered familiar face on the Puss-in-Boots Guy. The way Precious had sniffed my jacket and sleeve and then given those awful interrogating yowls—every time, it had been after an encounter with the kids. After the kids had been crowding around me. Plastering their sticky little hands all over my jacket and sleeves. He'd scented them on me. He'd been trying to ask me about them. Trying desperately to communicate with me. To find a way back where he belonged. Where he was happy. He *was* their cat. I knew that now, beyond any doubt. He wasn't Precious, he was Champ from Peckham.

Vaguely, I was aware of movement at both ends of the Main Aisle. The Inspector and a couple of his men were approaching from one end of the aisle. At the other end, rounding the corner midway between Dave's stand and the Big Cage, Carlotta, Roger Chesne-Malvern and Hugo Verrier were approaching. They hadn't seen each other yet, our group was in the middle, blocking their view. They advanced on us from both sides.

Across the aisle, the carpenters tossed the last of the guard rails into the pile on the ground and moved off, presumably to begin dismantling the unoccupied aisles of the rest of the Exhibition while they waited for us to leave. I wondered how much longer the Inspector would keep us—and whether he'd like to sort out this little mess. He'd been worried about whether or not I had made off with Pandora. Here was a genuine catnapping for him to solve.

'You know,' Kellington Daszco said abruptly, 'that

cat looks happy. It's the first time I've seen him when he wasn't trying to tear the place apart.'

'He knows us,' the boy said. 'He belongs to us. He wants to go home with us.'

'Yes,' Helena said softly, 'perhaps he does.' She released the other boy, who moved up to stand beside his brother. The little girl smiled up at me and went over with them.

'You can't *do* this,' Marcus Opal said wildly. 'You can't take him away from me. He's mine—mine! What right have they to him? They don't even know what they have. You can't leave a jewel on a dung-heap. It belongs to the person who recognizes it for what it is—not to the fool who threw it there. Precious Black Jade is *mine!*'

The kids were surrounding the cat, one with a throttlehold on his neck, another tugging fondly at a dangling hind leg, the little girl patting his head rather heavily. Yet that snarling, battling spitfire hung there, offering no resistance. On his face there was an expression of foolish resignation. A loud, unfamiliar throbbing pulsed out from his throat.

Champ was purring.

Marcus seemed to know that he had lost. 'I couldn't resist,' he wailed. 'He was so beautiful, so perfect, just what I had been looking for. Why shouldn't I? I took better care of him than they ever could. I fed him better, housed him better, provided him with a mate, gave him every luxury—'

'Alas,' Kellington sighed, 'he loved not wisely, but too well.'

It seemed to be the opinion of them all. Helena smiled at him sympathetically and then, over my shoulder, at Roger, who had joined us.

It was impossible not to feel sorry for Marcus. You could tell yourself that he didn't deserve it, that he was a thief—but he was so crazy about that cat. I wondered, if I had the chance to tuck Pandora under my jacket and sneak away with sporting odds against being caught, how far I could be trusted myself.

'You've still got Topaz,' I tried to comfort him, holding the little golden cat out to him.

'No.' He took her automatically, stroking her sadly. 'She's gone too. Beyond my reach. She's lovely—but what use is a little queen without the perfect stud?'

Carlotta and Hugo had stopped beside the Big Cage, they seemed to be arguing. The Inspector was abreast of us now.

'Excuse me, sir,' he called out, 'we'd like to speak to you again. Just a formality. If you'd come along with us.'

'Yes, of course.' Roger Chesne-Malvern smiled and stepped forward.

'No, sir, not you,' the Inspector said. 'Verrier—I mean—Mr Verrier, is the one we want.'

Hugo looked down the aisle at us all, and moved back. He still kept a hold on Carlotta's arm and she moved with him. She didn't seem to like it, she said something sharply to him.

He struck her across the face. While we still goggled, he swung her around in front of him like a shield.

'Now, just come along quietly,' the Inspector said, in tones of sweet reasonableness. 'You can't do yourself any good by behaving like this.'

'Come and get me!' Hugo challenged. He lurched up against the Big Cage. I saw the swift, blurred motion of his hand, as he pulled at something. Then, for good measure, he kicked the cage.

The Inspector wasn't as familiar with the set-up as the rest of us. He didn't realize what had happened. Intent on Hugo, he had not seen the door at the end of the cage slide upwards.

Advancing, he stopped suddenly at finding his path to Hugo blocked by two Sumatran tigers.

Chapter

15

'*Stay still!*' Carlotta shouted. 'Oh, please, do not anybody move.'

The humans didn't need telling, but the cats scented danger and scattered. Animated chunks of fur flew through the air and lit out for what they considered safety. Pandora, I was glad to see, was a real little PR cat. At the first sign of trouble, she was going to pretend she wasn't there and hope it would pass over her head without noticing her. She sent me a look of frantic innocence—that was one cage door *she* hadn't opened—and went to ground under the table.

One cat miscalculated. A silver idiot ran directly up the aisle towards the tigers, catching their attention. One great paw swung out and the white cat went flying through the air to land somewhere behind Carlotta and Hugo. Betty Lington screamed sharply and began sobbing. She tried to move forward, but Helena Keswick caught her arm.

'It's too late to do anything,' Helena said. 'It won't help if they kill you, too.'

'Please!' Carlotta struggled against Hugo. 'Let me go. Let me talk to Pyramus and Thisbe. I must calm them. They are overwrought—it is dangerous. They must return to their cage.'

'That's the idea, my pet.' Hugo continued backing slowly, pulling Carlotta with him. 'Let the nice policemen put them back in their cage. We're leaving.'

'You're under arrest!' the Inspector snapped at him. It was a pretty good try. Especially for a raging aureliophobe who was caught up in what must be every aureliophobe's most secret nightmare, standing his ground before a pair of cats weighing at least 350 pounds each.

The tigers seemed bewildered at being out of their cage and faced with so much light and space. One, on hearing Carlotta's voice, had turned that way and seemed to be considering going to her. The other was facing the Main Aisle squarely and obviously didn't like the sight. The terrible challenging scream sounded again. Then the tiger began to pad forward slowly.

'For God's sake,' Marcus Opal shouted, 'can't you shoot him?'

'Don't be a fool,' Kellington snapped. 'You know our police don't carry guns.'

'Then hit it with a truncheon,' Marcus insisted. (I'd like to have seen him try it and so, obviously, would the Inspector.) 'Where's your truncheon?'

'We don't carry them any more.' The Inspector's eyes swivelled viciously towards Marcus—if he could have turned that look on the tiger, he might have had a sporting chance of stunning it. 'They issue us with walkie-talkies these days, sir.'

Now that he mentioned it, I recognized the crackling noise in the background—I'd thought it was my nervous system breaking up. From the commotion issuing from it, I gathered Headquarters was tuned in to us and knew what was happening.

'How long will it take help to get here?' I asked the Inspector.

'They'll be here as soon as possible, sir,' he said. Which translated, as we all knew, into 'Too long.'

I was nearest the Inspector and could pick up occasional words squawking over the box. Words

like, 'Whipsnade', 'RSPCA' and 'Regent's Park'. By
the time they rallied their forces and found animal
trainers competent to deal with the situation, we
could all be mincemeat.

'You mean there's nothing we can do except stand
here and wait?' Marcus protested.

'If you're a religious man, you might try praying,'
the Inspector said.

'I'd rather try a double brandy,' Gerry murmured.

The tiger had stopped advancing and had half-
turned to look back at his mate. She was still
watching Carlotta and Hugo with a great deal of
interest. My own view wasn't too good but, from
what I could see, I didn't blame her.

For a man who wanted to get away so urgently,
Hugo was behaving in an extraordinary manner. He
had stopped by Dave Prendergast's stand and, still
shielding himself with Carlotta, had taken the new
shovel and was prodding it into the thick carpet of
Pussy No-Poo beneath the roots of each tree.

Carlotta had gone very quiet after her first out-
break. Hugo had either half-strangled her, or she had
decided that she was in the hands of a raving lunatic.
Either way, she was offering no resistance, despite
the fact that he was only holding her with one arm.
Although, if he had done much sculpting, he must
have arms as strong as a blacksmith's.

The other tiger moved back a few paces and
seemed undecided as to whether or not he wanted to
join his mate. She had inched forward slightly, still
watching Carlotta. Carlotta was watching her, too,
but there was no hint in either face of what they
might be thinking.

It was so silent, barring the crackle from the
walkie-talkie, that we heard the 'thunk' as the shovel
struck something solid. Hugo pulled up the tilting
sapling, tossed it aside, and then tried to use the
shovel as a lever to raise his find.

By then, we all knew, or guessed, what he must be

after. A golden head rose into view as the chemical turf slid away. As Marcus had been saying, a jewel on a dungheap indeed.

'We know all about it, Verrier,' the Inspector said. 'The whole insurance fraud you planned. Just come along quietly.' They were fairly brave words from a man who wasn't going anywhere himself just yet. 'You can't get away with it.'

'So that was it,' Helena Keswick said. 'He stole his own statue to collect the insurance money. And then, I suppose, he intended to melt it down and use the gold again. Or just sell the gold. But Rose—'

'Rose was upset about something.' Roger Chesne-Malvern was grim. 'She hadn't time to explain, but I gathered it was partly to do with her emerald earrings, and partly to do with the amount the statue had been insured for.'

'That's right,' Helena said. 'We were all rather surprised when we learned the amount. It was higher than we had thought.'

'Precisely,' the Inspector said. 'Mrs Chesne-Malvern had planned on a smaller sum. She was only thinking of it from the publicity angle, she hadn't intended to realize on the policy. After the theft, when the insurance adjuster interviewed her and she learned the actual amount of the policy for the first time, she began to be suspicious. I presume that she took the matter up with Verrier. That was the night he killed her.'

'It was an accident,' Hugo shouted. 'I was trying to reason with her. She wouldn't listen. It was her own fault. I pushed her and she fell. She hit her head on the corner of this stand. She was dead when I picked her up.'

'Was she?' The Inspector was completely deadpan. 'You thought the guard was dead, too, didn't you? That's why you left him there without finishing the job.' It could have been, it probably was, a bluff. But my blood ran cold.

'She was dead!' Hugo screamed. 'She was! And I

couldn't leave her lying there—someone might investigate the stand. I had to get her out of the way—distract attention from the stand until I had time to get the statue away—so . . . so, I . . .' he faltered to a halt. It was hard to rationalize what he had done next. Even though it had obviously appeared to be a logical step to him at the time.

One good thing was coming out of all this. Big cats, it seemed, were just as curious as their smaller brethren. Hugo's ranting had riveted their attention. I was not the only person, I noticed, to take advantage of this fact by slowly edging away from the centre of the aisle. Most of us were gradually retreating, in slow motion, to the comparative safety of what had been our stalls. Although, with the guard rails gone, the security they offered was purely imaginary.

Only the Inspector stood firm. It was kinder to think that than to assume that he was frozen there. Besides, he was between us and the Big Cats—any movement by him might have drawn their attention.

'You let Pyramus and Thisbe take the blame!' For the first time, Carlotta spoke. 'You deliberately plotted that they should be accused. It did not matter to you that you put them in danger of being killed as rogue animals.' Her eyes blazed dangerously, but Hugo could not see them.

'Why should I care, you stupid cow?' He gave her a shake. 'Shut up and keep out of this!'

'Thisbe!' Carlotta said quietly, and she added something very quickly in Spanish.

The tigress raised her head, listening, then started forward with an air of determination.

'Stop her!' Hugo pulled at Carlotta. 'Make her go back. I warn you—you'll regret it.'

Carlotta stayed silent. Her face contorted as Hugo twisted her arm. Thisbe continued advancing.

'Go back!' Hugo screamed. 'Go away!' He brandished the shovel at the tigress.

Thisbe ignored him. She took her orders from Carlotta. She padded forward, waiting for the next command. She was close enough to claw them now. Hugo panicked.

Leaning around Carlotta, he struck out with the shovel. It caught the tigress on her sensitive nose and one side of her mouth.

With a shriek of agonized rage, the tigress sprang backwards. Landing, she backed still farther away, growling furiously. I was suddenly very glad that I hadn't been the one to infuriate her.

Still holding Carlotta in front of him, Hugo scrabbled wildly to pull the gold Whittington Cat out of its hiding-place. He kept both eyes on Thisbe, who was crouched, growling, glaring at him.

Hugo hauled the gold cat with the emerald eyes up into the crook of his arm. So far, so good. But he no longer had just the police—who must worry about the safety of the others in the Hall as much as bringing a criminal to book—to contend with. His principal stumbling block now was Thisbe, who recognized no other consideration than the injury he had done to her.

Thisbe ran forward a couple of feet and crouched again, tail lashing, growls rising.

Deadly adversaries, they watched each other. Trying to assess the mood, the timing, the intention, lying behind each other's eyes.

'Call her off!' Hugo ordered Carlotta. 'Call her off!' Carlotta was silent. Perhaps Hugo was the only one present who did not realize that Thisbe was beyond control now. If Carlotta tried to stop the tigress, she would only undermine what authority she had over the animal.

Thisbe gathered herself and hurled into forward movement. Hugo screamed, and threw Carlotta into her path.

But he had miscalculated. Had Thisbe been intending a dash at him, Carlotta would have met the tigress head-on. But Thisbe sprang.

Recognizing her intention, Carlotta dived to the floor and spread herself flat. The tigress cleared her easily and landed on Hugo.

One final scream was all he had time for. The gold statue dropped from his arms and rolled along the floor.

'Really!' Into the abrupt silence, Kellington Dasczo spoke Hugo's epitaph. 'If you *will* hit a tigress on an abscessed tooth, what do you expect? It was a most uncomfortable way of committing suicide.'

Automatically, the Inspector started towards the scene. He stopped when he saw that the movement had focused the attention of Pyramus on him. The big tiger swung slowly towards us. His mate was doing just fine, and wanted no interference from bystanders. He was going to mount guard and see that she wasn't disturbed.

Personally, I wouldn't have dreamed of disturbing her. Not for the world. Hugo had bought it, fairly and squarely. In fact, I agreed with Kellington Dasczo—it was a suicide.

Now that I thought it over—and I much preferred to concentrate on that, rather than watch what Thisbe was doing—she had been giving every indication that something was wrong with her. All those roars and growls, the way she gnawed her meat so cautiously, on one side of her mouth only—perhaps we ought to have spotted it before.

The growling was diminuendo now. Thisbe raised her head and looked around, as though puzzled. She pawed at the broken bleeding heap on the ground a couple of times, but it didn't move again, and she lost interest. She turned away. For her, the incident was over.

'Thisbe . . . Thisbe . . . querida . . .' Slowly, Carlotta glided toward the tigress, murmuring coaxingly in

Spanish. Thisbe, tail still lashing restlessly, watched her advance. No one else dared move.

Carlotta's eyes were sparkling as she challenged the big cat. I realized that she was enjoying herself. In a way, it was understandable. When a woman's formative years had been spent as the lynchpin of a Revolution, what does she do for an encore? Some people are never happy unless they're putting themselves in one firing line or another.

'Thisbe . . .' Thisbe went to Carlotta. I think we were all holding our collective breath, but Thisbe's flash of temper was over. She had no grudge against Carlotta, who had never harmed her.

Carlotta led her gently back to the cage. As she walked past the head of the aisle, we could see the swelling on her jaw. It was now large enough to be noticeable, and would probably be the source of her reprieve. A dose of chloroform and a good vet, and Carlotta could convince the authorities that Thisbe's nature was again as sweet as it had ever been.

Pyramus had been moving docilely, following Thisbe towards the cage. It looked as though our troubles were over. Relief made the Inspector reckless.

'Let's clear up this mess,' he snapped to the constable. They started forward.

Pyramus whirled abruptly. They froze again. Carlotta glanced at them helplessly, but all her being was concentrated on persuading Thisbe into the cage. She would have to come back for Pyramus after that.

Pyramus wasn't waiting for her. Growling, tail lashing, he moved towards the Inspector. He paused and roared the ear-splitting challenge again.

A lighter, softer, but equally furious challenge sounded from behind us, farther down the aisle. I turned to see with horror that Mother Brown had taken up a stance in the centre of the aisle.

Back arched, tail bushed, hair bristling, that poor,

crazy, gallant little cat was ready to take on a tiger in defence of her kittens.

What else could I do? As Pyramus started forward, I snatched up the sculptor's stand, sending the photograph flying. Holding the stand in front of me, I tried to block Pyramus's advance.

I had only a few seconds of regretting the pretentious black velvet draped around the stand, which made it more awkward to manage. Then a swipe from Pyramus's paw tore the velvet away and sent it flying after the photograph.

The tiger stood staring at the four legs of the stand, as though puzzled at the way a human could suddenly grow such strange appurtenances. Since he had stopped moving forward, I decided to see if I could urge him backward, on the principle that every few feet farther away he got from the women and children would give them a better chance of escaping.

'Get back! Back!' I jabbed the metal legs at him tentatively. He was a great, powerful beast. If he took another swing and connected with that rigid metal, I stood a good chance of getting a broken arm as the sculptor's stand was torn from my grasp.

Pyramus growled and retreated a few inches. Injudiciously, I feinted with the spidery metal legs again. 'Back!'

This time he decided on action. He lunged and his teeth closed over one leg. He gnawed at it, growling viciously, then seemed surprised at the resistance his teeth encountered. He also seemed vaguely surprised that I was still standing, instead of falling before his attack.

I began to understand why animal trainers used chairs. That beast thought the sculptor's stand was an extension of me—part of me. There he was, doing his level best to gnaw a chunk off of me, and I seemed unharmed. It began to shake his confidence. It occurred to me that I could shake it a bit more.

'Back!' I shoved the stand at him. The end of the leg already in his mouth slipped a little farther in. It must have seemed to him that I was trying to jam it down his throat. Perhaps I might have, if I thought I stood a chance of succeeding.

He snarled and retreated again, to ease the pressure against the back of his throat. Then retreated still farther, to spit the thing out of his mouth altogether.

'Good boy, Douglas, you've got him going!' Kellington was doing more than simply cheering me on. Out of the corner of my eye, I saw that he had caught up Pearlie King's three-legged stool. Holding it in front of him, he closed in beside me on the left.

Gerry grabbed the pitchfork from Dave and moved in on my right. I was protected on both flanks now, and began to feel slightly better about the situation. I would still rather have been practically anywhere else in the world at the moment; but, at least, I didn't feel quite so naked now.

'Keep moving,' Kellington directed. 'It's the footwork that does it—I've watched a lot of animal acts. Always keep them moving, so that they can't get enough balance to spring, and you're all right.'

I wished I could be as sure of that as he sounded. But it was no time for arguing.

Thisbe was safely inside the cage, and Carlotta stood by the door of the cage, ready to raise it again when we had Pyramus into position to manoeuvre into it. She called out something encouragingly. But as it was in Spanish, I couldn't tell whether she was trying to encourage us or the tiger.

We moved forward slowly in unison. Before the combined onslaught, Pyramus fell back. Unfortunately, he seemed likely to back into the Inspector, who was still in the centre of the aisle, by the cage.

'I'd move out of the way, old chap, if I were you,'

Gerry called out. It seemed to break the spell. The Inspector found that he could move after all—and move pretty fast. He got half-way up the winding iron staircase leading to the Press Gallery before he stopped. He seemed to feel safe there, and we were too occupied to tell him that big cats have no more trouble climbing steps than small cats.

We were at the head of the aisle now, backing Pyramus around the corner, when he decided on another show of strength. He gave a snarling roar and lashed out with a paw. It snapped one leg off Kellington's stool and sent it hurtling to land at the foot of the Press Gallery staircase. The Inspector flinched.

But we all still kept moving, and the fact seemed to rattle Pyramus. He backed away, growling. Carlotta spoke again and he turned to her. She pulled at the chain and the cage door slid upwards.

With a last, hunted glare at us, Pyramus turned and rushed into the cage, where he knew he would be safe from the problems he was meeting in the cold, cruel world outside. Carlotta let the door drop shut swiftly.

It was over—and we were still alive. We lowered our defensive weapons and grinned at each other shakily.

'Shall we,' Kellington said, 'draw straws to see who gets to faint first?'

Chapter

16

One by one, the cats crept back into view. Pandora surfaced first, delicately stepping over the hamper, yawning and stretching, as though she had simply dropped off for a while. Pearlie King paused to sharpen his claws on a chunk of railing, as though in readiness to go into battle. Champ and Topaz emerged from under the same table, looking unconcerned. It was amazing the way every one of those cats managed to give the impression that they had simply had better things to do during the recent unpleasantness than attempt to join in. I realized that all cats were born PR characters—perhaps it was due to be their next incarnation. Or had been their last.

The owners swooped on their respective cats. Helena Keswick was nuzzling Mother Brown with a display of affection I no longer thought excessive. I discovered that I was nose-deep in Pandora's fur, myself. It occurred to me that it was time I did something about regularizing our position.

Roger Chesne-Malvern was with Helena. I started towards him, then turned back. 'Gerry,' I said apologetically, 'I know it's a small flat, but—'

'I saw it coming,' he said resignedly. 'I warned you. That's a very expensive bit of fluff—she'll be mainlining caviar in no time at all.'

'Not if some sneak doesn't introduce her to it,' I said.

'All right, have it your own way,' he said. 'You will, anyway. Heaven help you the day some woman gets her hooks into you—you've no sales resistance at all.'

'Thanks, Gerry.' I went over to Roger Chesne-Malvern. Then I was completely tongue-tied. How do you ask a man if he'll sell his late wife's cat to you, but allow you to postdate the cheque until you're sure her cheque to your Company has cleared?

'. . . six months is plenty,' he was saying to Helena. 'Damn it, we're not living in Victorian times.' He looked up abruptly, and there was no time to retreat.

I cleared my throat and plunged in. 'I was wondering,' I said, 'if you'd consider selling Pandora—?'

'No.' He smiled, but shook his head firmly. 'I wouldn't dream of selling Pandora.'

Of course I had known that she was a very valuable cat. 'In that case . . .' I tried to hand her over, but he waved her away.

'Later,' he said, 'there's plenty of time.' He bent to Helena again, and there was nothing for me to do but move away.

The Inspector was waiting by Pandora's stall. Penny and Gerry were sitting there talking to him. Little Topaz perched on our table beside Pandora's pen.

A lesser man than the Inspector would have fabricated some urgent excuse for getting back to Headquarters immediately. The Inspector had a flimsy excuse for staying, but I could read the truth in his eyes: he was determined to lick this thing. He had faced the worst he could possibly face, and now he was going up again immediately—before he lost his nerve.

'I thought I'd let you know,' he said. His hand danced out tentatively towards Pandora and pulled back again. 'You can all go now. Of course, you'll hold yourselves ready to give statements. But tomorrow will be time enough.' His hand feinted towards Pandora again, but the memory of her temper obviously intervened. His nerve cracked.

Topaz sat, placid and blinking, on the table. He settled for her, instead. 'Nice little cat,' he said, and forced his fingers into contact with the top of her head.

Topaz blinked at him and obligingly purred. His confidence grew. 'Very nice little cat.' He let his hand settle on her head and sweep down towards her back. Then he jerked his hand away abruptly.

'That cat is soaking wet,' he said accusingly.

Sure enough, she was. 'Why, you little devil!' I said. She rolled large golden eyes at me and blinked complacently.

'I think that's all,' the Inspector said. Honour was satisfied. He didn't have to *like* the brutes—but they no longer had him on the run. 'Good night.' He took a deep breath and tapped the top of Pandora's head. She didn't react one way or another. He beamed and walked jauntily away. A man without phobias. It was a kill or cure treatment, but it had been cure. I didn't think it was practical to patent it, though.

Gerry had seen Roger Chesne-Malvern wave me away. He preserved a discreet silence. So did Penny, he must have signalled her. It didn't make me feel any better.

Next door, the kids had Precious Champ back in their collective stranglehold. He lolled there in their arms with an expression of beatified resignation. He was going home, and he knew it. For the first time, we were looking at a happy cat—he bore no resemblance to the vicious neurotic wreck who had been snarling his way through the Exhibition. That alone would have told anyone where he belonged—and where he wanted to be.

Marcus had surrendered unconditionally. He was

now begging his own kind of mercy from the victors.
'You must take his bowl, and his brush, and his
chamois cloth—you must rub his coat with the
chamois after you brush him. It polishes his fur,
gives it lustre, brings out the highlights. And his
carrying case—you can't take him on public trans-
port like that. You ought to take a taxi. Would you let
me give you the money for a taxi?'

Three pairs of eyes consulted each other. Marcus
beamed in on the little girl as perhaps the most
vulnerable. 'Here's five pounds,' he pleaded. 'That
should take you home in a taxi—and leave you some
change. You can keep the change. Buy him—buy
him something nice with it. Salmon, perhaps—he's
very partial to a bit of fresh salmon. Poached lightly
in cream.'

She accepted the money with a sweet smile. From
what I'd seen of that kid, it would go straight into a
benevolent fund for herself, with a small unavoid-
able percentage being shared with her brothers.
Champ would get baked beans on toast—and be
happy with it. 'All right,' she said.

'Thank you, thank you,' Marcus Opal nearly wept.
'May I . . . just pat him . . . one last time . . . ?'
He stretched out his hand.

Precious tensed, recoiled, snarled, and lashed out.
A long scarlet slash appeared along the back of
Marcus's hand. It looked deep enough to leave a scar.
Precious had given him something to remember him
by—permanently.

Before they left in triumph, the little girl came over
and clutched my sleeve. 'Thank you, Mr Perkins,'
she said gravely. 'Thank you very much.'

'That's all right, sweetheart.' I patted the top of her
head.

'Really!' Penny sniffed, looking after them. 'I don't
know how you *could*. Anyone can see she's common
as dirt!' I did a doubletake. It was ridiculous, but she

sounded almost jealous. Little Penny—but that was silly.

Betty Lington was sobbing in the background. 'Oh, Silly . . . oh, Silver . . .' over and over. The police had taken the mangled little body away, only allowing her the briefest glimpse of it. I suspected they were trying to spare her from seeing the full extent of the damage, but she had seen enough. 'Oh, Silly . . .'

Dave Prendergast approached her diffidently. 'Here's her ribbon. It fell off by my stand. I thought you might like to have it.' He held a tattered scrap of blue satin out to her.

Betty Lington looked up and screamed. A dusty pink nose, in a grime-streaked fur face, was emerging slowly from beneath a pile of railing and carpenters' tools. Eyes rolling wildly, still doubting the wisdom of ever coming into the daylight again, Silver Fir inched into view. More grey and black than silver, right now.

'Silly! Silly!' Betty Lington pounced on her. 'You're all right! You're safe. Clever, clever girl!' Silver Fir sank bonelessly into her arms, shivering. Her eyes were cloudy and worried. For the first time, she had dimly comprehended that there might be another world beyond the bright lights, the talcum powder and the cameras. There was a jungle out there somewhere—and she did not like her encounter with it.

'Then who—?' Dave looked at the scrap of blue ribbon.

'Lady Purr-fect,' I realized. The anonymous, interchangeable cat. The carpenters must have unlatched her pen when they were fooling around her. And Lady Purr-fect, Mark V version, had not been on exhibit long enough to know the lie of the land. All the other cats had been out of their pens frequently, cuddling in their owners' arms, looking around, able to see the set-up. None of them had made the mistake of heading straight into the danger zone. The admass puss was the only one not clued in. But no one would worry—she belonged to the agency, and there were four more duplicates, each as photogenic as the other. Poor little characterless cat.

'I'm glad.' Marcus Opal was standing beside us, trying not to look at Topaz. A very sensible precaution, and one I ought to emulate.

'Goodbye, doll.' I pulled open the door of the pen and tossed Pandora inside. There was no point in prolonging the agony. We had other clients, other promotions coming up—I could throw myself into my work and, before long, I wouldn't remember her at all—or only very vaguely.

"I'm so glad—' Marcus dabbed at his bleeding hand with a handkerchief dipped in antiseptic—'her cat is safe. We've had enough tragedies here. One less—'

He broke off as Topaz rose and advanced. She sniffed at his hand, then rubbed her head against it. 'No.' Visibly, Marcus tried to harden his heart. 'No, there's no sense to it now. Go away.'

Topaz looked up at him, with that bright uncritical gaze. She, at least, adored him. She saw no fault in him. She would happily be his cat.

'No, please,' Marcus said faintly.

'It's worth a chance.' I helped the weakening process. 'She was under that table with Precious for quite a while. And the back of her neck was all wet.'

'Really?' He glanced at me brightly, then checked the damp fur for himself.

'If I were a bookie, I'd give you odds,' I said.

'Precious did seem terribly taken with her.' Marcus cheered up immediately. 'Perhaps it is worth a chance.' He bustled off with her, to settle up with her owner.

I tried not to notice that Roger and Helena had come up behind me. Helena was packing Pandora's clobber into a basket, and Roger was coaxing Pandora into her carrying case.

I didn't watch them. At the same time, I saw why none of the cat-lovers had taken too hard a line with Marcus. *He loved not wisely, but too well*, did indeed express it for them. But now he had a second chance. One queen was already in kitten to Precious—his perfect stud—and it was practically a dead cert that Topaz was, too. Marcus Opal would have his Precious Jewel Cattery, after all. Breeding the best of the kittens back to their dams, he could build up the strain and develop a fine bloodline. Perhaps he didn't deserve it—or perhaps he did. *Much has been forgiven thee, because thou hast loved much.* Who knows?

I looked around. There was no one else to say goodbye to. Kellington had left earlier, but we were meeting for lunch next week. It was probably the beginning of a lifelong friendship. Once you've been under fire, sharing the same foxhole, you know what the other guy is really made of.

Gerry and Penny were waiting for me. 'Come on,' I said to them, and to Dave, who was still pensively fingering the shredded ribbon, 'I'll buy us all a drink.'

'Just a minute,' Roger Chesne-Malvern said. I turned, and he held the carrying case out to me. 'Don't forget your cat.'

'But . . . I thought . . . I mean . . .' I was stammering.

'No, I wouldn't dream of *selling* her.' He smiled. 'But she's yours. Haven't you ever heard that "You don't choose a cat, a cat chooses you?" Pandora is a free spirit, and it has been very plain for quite some time that she prefers your company.

'Mr Perkins, you have a cat. Speak now, or for ever hold your peace.'

'Prrryow!' Pandora nagged sharply.

'All right.' I snatched the carrying case before he could change his mind. 'Thank you. Thanks—'

Penny closed in and collected the basket with all Pandora's things in it. Helena smiled her slow, catlike smile. Pandora might be going, but there would be no lack of cats in Roger Chesne-Malvern's home life from now on.

'Come on,' Gerry urged. 'This is going to be a *real* celebration now.'

'All right,' I agreed, 'we'll have a few drinks at the pub. And then,' I said to Pandora, 'we're going home.'

ABOUT THE AUTHOR

MARIAN BABSON is the author of more than twenty-five mysteries. Winner of the Poisoned Chalice and Sleuth awards, she was also a nominee for the British Gold and Silver Dagger awards. She is listed in *Publishers Weekly* as one of today's best British mystery writers. She lives in London.

BANTAM MYSTERY COLLECTION

Kinsey Millhone is...

"The best new private eye." —*The Detroit News*

"A tough-cookie with a soft center." —*Newsweek*

"A stand-out specimen of the new female operatives."
—*Philadelphia Inquirer*

Sue Grafton is...

The Shamus and Anthony Award winning creator of Kinsey Millhone and quite simply one of the hottest new mystery writers around.

- [ ] 27991 "A" IS FOR ALIBI $3.95
- [ ] 28034 "B" IS FOR BURGLAR $3.95
- [ ] 28036 "C" IS FOR CORPSE $3.95
- [ ] 27163 "D" IS FOR DEADBEAT $3.95
- [ ] 27955 "E" IS FOR EVIDENCE $3.95
- [ ] 28478 "F" IS FOR FUGITIVE $4.50